Jeremy Carter:
The Swell of Hope and Fury

LIOR ZELERING

First published 2025
by Rowanvale Books Ltd
The Gate
Keppoch Street
Roath
Cardiff
CF24 3JW
www.rowanvalebooks.com

A CIP catalogue record for this book is available from the British Library.
Paperback ISBN: 978-1-83584-120-4
eBook ISBN: 978-1-83584-121-1

*DEDICATED TO HANNAH
AND AMRAM ZELERING*

Contents

Chapter 1

The waves were perfect—smooth, glassy, and rolling in one after the other like gifts from the ocean. They formed clean lines that glimmered under the early-morning sun, each swell peaking at just the right moment. The sun hung lazily over Crescent Bay, painting the sky in soft streaks of orange and pink. From his vantage point just beyond the break, Jeremy Carter perched on his surfboard, bobbing with the rhythm of the tide, waiting for the next set to roll in. He didn't live for much, but he lived for this. Out here, with salt on his skin and an endless horizon in front of him, life felt easy. No drama, no deadlines, no stress—just the ocean and him, moving as one.

Jeremy's unruly blond hair, still damp from his last wave, clung to his forehead. He brushed it back while scanning the distance. The buzz of conversation from beachgoers was a faint backdrop—mere static compared to the soundtrack of crashing waves and seagulls. He could make out a few families settling on towels and setting up umbrellas near the shore, though their chatter was muffled by the breeze.

Then a promising swell appeared on the horizon, rising steadily. Jeremy's pulse quickened. He paddled with smooth, practiced strokes, arms propelling him forward in a time-honored ritual. As the wave caught him, he pushed to his feet in a single fluid motion, knees instinctively bending to center his balance. For a brief, electric moment, he felt like he was flying as his board sliced across the face of the wave, carving a graceful line.

"Yewww!" he hollered, letting out a rush of adrenaline as he shifted his weight for a casual carve to the left. *Style is everything*, he reminded himself. He saw a tube forming just ahead—a gorgeous, translucent curl—and his heart pounded.

I gotta drill this one, he thought, angling his board to line up perfectly. Water arced over him, forming a shimmering tunnel of light and ocean. Adrenaline flooded his veins as he entered the tube, the roar of water enveloping him like a cocoon. For a few seconds, time slowed. Then he burst out into open air, triumphant.

"Heck, yeah," he muttered to himself, already imagining how this ride would score in a real competition. A 9.2, maybe even higher with a perfectly executed tube like that. But out here, there was no panel of judges. It was just him and the ocean. As he glided back onto the shore, dripping and grinning, a couple of kids on the sand offered a smattering of applause.

"Sick ride, Carter!" one of them shouted.

Jeremy answered with a laid-back shaka sign as he grabbed his towel. The day had barely started, but he felt like he'd already accomplished something major. The sea was calm, the sky cloudless—what could possibly ruin such a perfect morning?

With a sigh, he remembered that life had a knack for intruding on perfection. Jeremy gathered his board, crossed the road to the nearby surf shop, and placed it beside his other belongings: a skateboard, a bit battered but beloved, leaning against his backpack. That board was his ride back to reality. School beckoned, along with all its mundane demands. Crescent Bay High wasn't far—just a short skate away. Part of him wanted to skip entirely and stay beachside, but he slung his bag over one shoulder, scooped up the skateboard, and headed off. Even if he wanted to dodge school forever, responsibilities had a way of catching up.

The skateboard rumbled under his feet as he rolled away from the beach. Salty ocean breeze still clung to the air, mingling with the faint smell of sunscreen and the asphalt that lay beneath his wheels. Jeremy wove around a parked car, one hand lightly gripping his backpack strap. Every movement was loose and effortless, like a dance he'd rehearsed a thousand times. Born into Californian surf-skate royalty, he came by it honestly: his grandfather, Roger "the Mule" Carter, was one of the first to slay giant waves, and his father, Chris Carter, carried that daredevil spirit from the ocean to the early '90s vert ramps. There was no denying that skateboarding and surfing were in Jeremy's blood.

He reached Crescent Bay High just as the sun climbed a bit higher in the sky. A lively chaos thrummed around the front gates. Clusters of students laughed, shouted, or trudged toward the entrance, some chugging energy drinks, others wearing earbuds and tuning out the world. The campus, surrounded by palm trees and aging brick walls, boasted a sign that read "Home of the Dolphins!" in bold letters. Even from outside, Jeremy could pick out the dull roar of conversation within the halls.

He kicked up the tail of his board and caught it with an easy motion, tucking it under his arm as he strolled inside. The chatter of the crowd surrounded him, a far cry from the meditative hush of the ocean. Lockers slammed, teachers barked reminders about homework, and friends called out to each other in passing. Jeremy had never loved these hallways. He found them confining—the exact opposite of what he experienced on a wave or skating the streets.

Still, he wore his usual lazy grin, hoping to coast through the day like he always did. He was just rounding the corner to his locker when he heard a voice behind him, one he could recognize even in his sleep.

"Jeremy!" The sharp tone cut through the corridor like a buzzer. He stopped in his tracks and turned to see Mrs. Simmons, his history teacher. She marched toward him with an air of suppressed impatience, a stack of papers tucked tightly under one arm.

The corners of Jeremy's mouth twitched in a lopsided smile. "Morning, Mrs. Simmons."

She didn't smile back. "Where's that essay I asked for last week?" She adjusted the papers in her arms, her expression expectant.

Jeremy gave her his most disarming grin, the one he'd perfected for exactly these situations. "I, uh ... left it at home. Totally finished it, though," he lied, scratching the back of his neck.

Mrs. Simmons's glare could have carved ice. "You mean the same essay you told me was 'almost done' three days ago?"

"Exactly. It's, uh … almost done at home." He shrugged, as if hoping the casual gesture would downplay the offense.

Her frown deepened, promising a lecture on personal responsibility. But before she could begin, Jeremy spotted an opening in the crowd. He flashed an apologetic wave and darted off, not waiting for her to continue. He heard her annoyed exclamation over the buzz of the hallway, but he pressed on. He might pay for it later, but that was future Jeremy's problem.

Skidding into the courtyard—a central square lined with picnic tables and patches of grass—Jeremy took a moment to catch his breath. The sun streamed in, illuminating dust motes that danced near the rafters. A scattering of students lounged at the tables, chatting or scrolling through their phones. This open-air spot was a mini-sanctuary, a place where he could breathe unfiltered air and maybe sneak in a daydream of surfing.

He'd taken no more than a few steps before the sight of three familiar figures made his stomach twist. Darren, the self-appointed king of campus cruelty, stood with his chest puffed out in his typical arrogant stance. Zack and Trevor flanked him like trained henchmen, always ready to snicker at Darren's every word or follow his lead. Jeremy's eyes tracked downward, where a smaller figure sat in a wheelchair, clutching a tablet. Lucas Chu.

Although Jeremy hardly knew Lucas personally, rumors of the kid's brilliance circulated around the school. People said he was on the verge of inventing the next big gadget or blueprint to change modern technology. That was the kind of potential that should earn respect, but apparently not in Darren's world. Right now, Darren was hovering over Lucas with a sneer on his face, holding Lucas's tablet just out of reach. Zack and Trevor chuckled like they were in the front row of a comedy show.

"What's the matter, Wheels? Gonna invent your way out of this?" Darren taunted, brandishing the tablet. Lucas's cheeks flushed. He reached for the device, but Darren sidestepped, keeping it out of range.

"C'mon, give it back." Lucas's voice was barely louder than a whisper, tension straining every syllable.

"What's that? Speak up, Einstein," Darren mocked, his smirk widening. Trevor intercepted the tablet when Darren tossed it, spinning around to keep it away from Lucas.

Jeremy hesitated. He wasn't a fan of bullies, but he also wanted no part in a scene like this. He was the kind of kid who kept his head down, mostly slipping under the radar unless he was on his board. Confronting Darren was just about the last thing he needed, especially since Darren and his football buddies were built like tanks. And yet, as he watched Lucas's face grow red with embarrassment and anger, something inside Jeremy snapped.

"Hey!" he yelled, louder than intended.

A sudden hush fell around them as all three bullies turned to stare at him. Even a few nearby students paused, sensing the sudden tension.

Jeremy forced himself to keep a cool posture. "How about you give that back and go find someone else to bother?" he said. His voice sounded steadier than he felt.

Darren's eyebrows rose, then a sneer curled his lips. "And who's gonna make me? You?" He eyed Jeremy's skateboard dismissively. "Why don't you take your little skateboard and flip out of here?"

Jeremy's grip on his board tightened. He was aware of how big Darren was, how the guy could probably flatten him if it came to a brawl. But a wave of anger surged in him, combined with just enough adrenaline and rebellious spirit to tip the balance.

Without another word, he swung his skateboard in a quick arc. The deck connected with Darren's jaw, eliciting a sharp crack that stunned everyone. Darren stumbled back, cupping his face with one hand.

"GET HIM!" he roared, eyes flaring with rage.

Jeremy didn't wait around. He dropped the skateboard, landed on it, and kicked off hard. The courtyard erupted in alarmed cries as students scrambled to clear a path. The wheels hummed against the pavement, drowning out everything but the pounding of his heart.

Behind him, Darren's voice echoed in raw fury, "GET HIM!" Zack and Trevor broke into a sprint. Jeremy risked a glance back, instantly regretting it. Darren was close, face twisted into a furious snarl, while Trevor elbowed a smaller kid away from a parked motorcycle. The kid yelled in protest, but Trevor only responded with a savage twist of the throttle. The engine roared, sending a shot of dread through Jeremy's veins.

"Oh, perfect," Jeremy muttered, pushing harder. The last thing he wanted was to outrun a motorcycle in a school courtyard, but there wasn't much choice.

He careened toward a flight of stairs leading to the lower level. An eight-stair. No big deal in a controlled environment, but now he was at top speed with adrenaline spiking. He crouched low, popped an ollie right at the edge, and soared for a split second, knees bending on impact to absorb the shock. He landed smoothly, thanks to hundreds of hours spent perfecting that motion. Applause and gasps merged into one sound behind him, but he didn't slow down.

Up at the top, Darren and Zack skidded to a halt. Darren shoved Zack forward, yelling, "WHAT ARE YOU WAITING FOR?!"

Trevor, meanwhile, avoided the stairs completely, steering the motorcycle around a different path. The engine's growl thundered in Jeremy's ears. He clenched his jaw. "Of course he's not taking the stairs like a normal person."

Spying a narrow walkway with a handrail, Jeremy lined himself up, heart hammering like mad. At the last second, he popped the tail of his board, locking his trucks onto the rail for a 50/50 grind. Sparks flew as metal scraped metal, eliciting excited shouts from a group of onlookers. He gritted his teeth and stayed balanced, the overhead rush igniting a flash of exhilaration in him. The moment he hit level ground again, he whooped, adrenaline buzzing.

"Yeah!" he yelled. But there was no time to celebrate. Trevor's motorcycle roared onto the walkway behind him, tires squealing. Zack and Darren had taken a side route, presumably trying to trap Jeremy from another angle.

The chase twisted around the school's cafeteria, where Jeremy dodged trash cans, benches, and startled students. He could almost feel Trevor's hot breath on his neck, though in truth it was just the roar of the motorcycle. Jeremy's eyes flicked around desperately, searching for a way out. He spotted a slab of broken pavement that angled upward—a makeshift ramp. Behind it yawned a long gap in the walkway.

He lined up the ramp, crouched low, and snapped an ollie, pulling his legs up midair. The board wobbled, so he instinctively grabbed it and tweaked his body into a style-heavy air Japan. Jeremy landed with a jarring thud, wheels rattling but holding firm, and rolled on. Behind him, Trevor skidded to a halt, cursing. The motorcycle wouldn't make that jump.

But as Jeremy pressed on, he realized he wasn't safe yet. The labyrinth of walkways behind Crescent Bay High connected to the gym and sports fields, twisting around in narrow corridors and low walls. Darren and Zack, no longer weighed down by the motorcycle's limitations, could still cut him off. Trevor's engine grumbled ominously in the distance, circling around for another angle.

Every fork in the path forced Jeremy to make a split-second decision. His heart pounded, sweat prickling his forehead. He had no plan—just instincts. He glimpsed a tall fence at the edge of campus. It marked the boundary between school property and a steep, rocky ditch plunging down into a patch of wilderness. The sun glinted off the chain-link, daring him to try something crazy.

Trevor roared into view from the left, the motorcycle's engine snarling. Darren and Zack reappeared to the right, each panting and red-faced but still determined. They were closing in fast, leaving Jeremy with only one escape route: the fence. He scanned the ground and spotted a sloped concrete bank leading straight toward it. If he timed his jump, he might sail over the fence, landing somewhere in that ominous ditch.

Why am I doing this? he thought fleetingly, adrenaline swirling with dread in his gut. Then Darren hollered an obscenity, spurring Jeremy into action.

He pushed hard, building speed. The bank approached faster than he liked. His muscles tensed, coiling like springs. Just as he hit the bank, he popped the tail and twisted his body into a frontside 180, turning midair to face the way he'd come. For a moment, he was weightless, flying high enough to clear the chain-link by a slim margin. The fence rushed under him.

He landed on the other side with bone-rattling force, knees absorbing the impact. The ground sloped sharply downward, sending him into the ditch at breakneck speed. Loose rocks crunched beneath his wheels. He heard Darren's shout, muffled by distance, and Trevor's furious cursing. The fence was too tall for them to clear so easily, especially with the motorcycle.

"YOU'RE DEAD, CARTER!" Darren's voice cracked as it ripped through the air.

Jeremy couldn't resist tossing a hasty salute over his shoulder. "Catch me later, losers!"

His attempt at bravado did little to calm the spike of fear thrumming in his chest. The ditch was worse than he'd anticipated—steeper and riddled with obstacles. Rocks jutted from the dirt in irregular patterns, and thick roots looped across the narrow path. Jeremy leaned back slightly, arms out for balance, trying to keep his board under control. The wheels churned up dust, the vibrations rattling his bones.

Beneath him, the slope twisted into sharp turns. One misstep and he'd be sprawling in the dirt with a broken arm, or worse. But Jeremy's focus snapped into high gear. Hours and hours of skating the rough streets around Crescent Bay High had trained him to adapt quickly. He zigzagged around protruding stones, hopped the worst of the roots, and clung to the board for dear life.

Finally, the ditch funneled into a narrow channel, leading to a dark, low tunnel. He glimpsed the figures of Darren and Zack up above, glaring over the fence, and heard Trevor revving the motorcycle in frustration.

Jeremy chuckled despite himself, adrenaline spiking so hard it made him feel giddy. The thick walls of the ditch enclosed him now, blocking out most of the light. Ahead, the tunnel beckoned like a black mouth. If he could just keep riding, maybe it would spit him out somewhere safe, far from Crescent Bay High.

He leaned forward, letting momentum carry him into the shadows. The roar of wind in his ears was deafening, and the cool air of the tunnel gave him goosebumps. In the darkness, the slope grew even steeper. Jeremy realized too late that the ground might be unstable. A rumble beneath his wheels made his heart lurch.

Suddenly, the floor gave way. Jeremy's skateboard skittered out from under him as the dirt crumbled, and he felt a lurch of pure fear. Everything was weightless. Rocks, chunks of concrete, and clouds of dust spun around him in a nightmarish blur. For an instant, the world seemed suspended, as if time itself had hit pause.

Then his shoulder struck something hard, and the air whooshed out of his lungs. The tunnel's collapsing floor dragged him deeper, tumbling him like clothes in a dryer. Pain flashed across his back, his arms, his ribs. Gravel scraped his palms. He had no sense of up or down anymore. There was only falling, spinning, and the unrelenting crush of debris.

Finally, he slammed onto a slanted surface with enough force to jar every bone in his body. He lay still, dust billowing all around him, the tunnel's darkness nearly absolute. He felt disoriented, battered, but for the moment, he was alive. Bits of rubble pattered around him, and the ground seemed to settle.

Everything was quiet, except for the rapid thud of his own heartbeat.

Chapter 2

Jeremy didn't remember hitting the ground. One moment, he was plummeting into a crumbling tunnel; the next, he woke up, coughing, on a hard surface. Dust clouded the air, pebbles clicking around him. His limbs felt as if they'd been run over by a truck— heavy, aching, and stiff. For a few stunned seconds, all he could do was lie there, gasping in shallow breaths.

Finally, he forced himself upright. Loose rocks cascaded off his jacket. He blinked, trying to orient himself. Where was he? The dull glow of moonlight, or maybe some other light, glimmered at the edges of his vision. The space felt huge, echoing every ragged inhalation. It was colder, too, the air laced with an odd metallic smell.

He scanned for his skateboard. Nothing. His heart sank. That board was practically an extension of his body—and now it was gone, lost in the chaos of the fall. Still, he had bigger problems. The tunnel above had collapsed, leaving him in what looked like a sprawling underground chamber.

What am I supposed to do?

He stood, legs unsteady, and took a few steps forward. That was when he noticed the walls: jagged rock fused with smooth, reflective surfaces, as though chunks of machinery were embedded in the stone. A subtle hum tingled at the edge of his hearing, and every now and then, a spark flickered along the ceiling, where thin wires coiled around stalactites in eerie loops.

"This is insane," Jeremy muttered. The place gave off a vibe somewhere between a natural cavern and a derelict sci-fi lab. He couldn't decide which possibility was more unsettling.

A faint light pulsed deeper within the cave, drawing him forward. He crept carefully over uneven ground. Glassy shards—iridescent in blues and greens—jutted from mounds of rubble. Some were bigger than car windows but curved like giant lenses. Others were small, cracked fragments. His thoughts spun: *How did any of this get under Crescent Bay?*

Gradually, the cavern widened into a massive central chamber. Fallen columns of rock and metal sprawled across the floor, as if something had shattered the space ages ago. In the middle, scorch marks fanned out in black rings, radiating from a single point. Jeremy's breath hitched when he saw what lay at the center: a diamond-like object, larger than a tennis ball, half-buried in the floor and glowing with shifting color.

He stepped closer, shoes crunching over broken debris. Even a few feet away, a gentle warmth emanated from the stone. It pulsed in a soft rhythm, almost like a heartbeat, cycling through luminous shades of blue, green, and silver. Wherever its light touched, the air shimmered faintly.

"What even is this?" he wondered, throat tightening as he spoke. It didn't look like any diamond he'd ever heard of—no hard edges, no obvious facets. Instead, it seemed organically smooth, more like a polished orb than a cut gemstone. And it was bigger than he first realized, definitely bulkier than a tennis ball, maybe the size of a large grapefruit.

As he stared, a thought pricked his mind: it felt *alive* somehow. The glow wasn't random; it was measured, pulsing like a living organism. Despite his fear, Jeremy found himself edging nearer. If this was a secret government project or some weird natural phenomenon, it was still mesmerizing.

His eyes drifted across its translucent surface. Within the swirling colors, he glimpsed shadowy shapes—suggestive of humanoid silhouettes—moving in the depths of the stone as though trapped behind tinted glass. Their outlines were distorted, arms and legs elongated. One seemed to turn its head toward him, faint light rippling around its form. A chill crawled up his spine.

Are they real, or is this just my brain messing with me?

He reached out, drawn as if compelled. "What are you?" he whispered.

The moment his fingertips grazed the stone, it exploded with brilliance, flooding the chamber with a dazzling burst of light. Jeremy staggered back, shielding his eyes. A roaring hum surged in his ears.

Visions slammed into his mind—too vivid to be dreams, too surreal to be reality. He saw galaxies spinning, stars being born and dying in silent supernovas. An endless ocean under a black, starless sky. Humanoid silhouettes appeared again, their bodies made of shimmering light, walking or standing in clusters as if they were waiting for something. Their faces were indistinct, but Jeremy sensed they looked right at him.

He felt a rush of energy surge through his veins, like hot electricity crawling under his skin. There was no pain, just an overwhelming sensation of fullness, as if he were a battery being charged far beyond capacity. The images came faster—too fast—blurring until he couldn't track them.

Then, as swiftly as it began, the light dimmed. His knees buckled. He dropped to the floor, panting in the sudden darkness. The diamond's glow had returned to its subdued pulsing.

After a few shaky breaths, he lifted his hand. A glowing mark now adorned his palm—a circular ripple pattern that flickered in the same shifting palette as the diamond. He flexed his fingers in disbelief. The glow didn't fade.

What the hell did that thing do to me? Jeremy's heart thudded like a jackhammer. He tried rubbing the mark away, but it stayed firmly on his skin, still pulsing in sync with the orb.

A low rumble broke the silence. The cavern floor trembled, sending shards of debris skittering.

"Oh, no," he breathed. Stone cracked overhead, and sparks rained down from the wiry coils on the ceiling. The diamond's glow flickered erratically, its once-steady heartbeat stuttering.

Without hesitation, Jeremy scrambled to his feet and bolted. He dashed back across the chamber, weaving around twisted columns. Rocks pummeled the ground, and the walls groaned under the strain. He nearly tripped over a chunk of metal paneling but managed to regain his balance. The corridor he'd come through was already collapsing in places, forcing him to duck under a jagged ledge.

The entire cavern roared, a final convulsion of stone and steel. Jeremy spotted moonlight—or maybe just night air—shining ahead, and he hurled himself toward it. His lungs burned, and panic threatened to clamp down on his chest, but adrenaline powered him forward.

He burst out into the open, stumbling across wet grass. Night engulfed him, calm and quiet compared to the catastrophe behind. Then came a thunderous crash as part of the cavern caved in. A cloud of dust whooshed out of the opening, making him cough and squint.

Gasping, Jeremy collapsed onto his knees. A few seconds later, the ground stopped shaking, leaving an eerie stillness. He peered back at the jagged hole in the hillside—nothing but darkness and settling debris. No sign of the glowing orb. No sign of the surreal half machinery.

Slowly, he flipped his hand over. The circular mark still glowed faintly in his palm, sending a soft tingle up his arm. He let out a shaky exhalation, mind spinning with everything he'd just experienced. That diamond—whatever it was—had given him a glimpse of something far beyond this world. And somehow, it had imprinted itself on him. He could still feel traces of that alien energy thrumming under his skin.

"What the hell is this?" he asked, voice trembling, as he stared at his hand. "I've never seen anything like it."

He had no idea how to explain any of this. To his left stood the tall fence encircling Crescent Bay High.

Darren, Zack, and Trevor had probably given up the chase hours ago, but no doubt they'd be bragging about the rampage. Meanwhile, Jeremy had discovered some freaky subterranean secret and ... possibly fused with a giant glowing diamond?

He rubbed grit from his eyes. The adrenaline was wearing off, replaced by bone-deep exhaustion and a throbbing bruise across his rib cage. He needed to get home, to shower, to sleep off the nightmare. If he told anyone, would they even believe him?

With a frustrated sigh, he stumbled toward the fence. Climbing it was an ordeal, every muscle shrieking in protest. He dropped into an empty back lot near the school's boundary, landing awkwardly. His gaze flicked to the horizon, searching for any sign of dawn. The sky was still dark, with just a hint of navy at the edges.

Walking through dimly lit streets, he hugged the shadows to avoid curious eyes. Normally, being this filthy would embarrass him, but he was too drained to care. As he approached his house, the porch light was off—a relief. He snuck around the side yard and hoisted himself through his bedroom window, stumbling onto the floor.

Dust coated his clothes and hair. He flicked on the smallest light in his room, wincing at his reflection in the mirror: dirt-streaked face, wide, haunted eyes, and that eerie glowing mark on his palm. He stared at the pattern—rippling, alive with shifting shades. In his mind's eye, he saw those humanoid silhouettes again, swirling galaxies reflecting in their luminous eyes.

What did I just sign up for?

He clenched his fist, trying to tamp down the wave of panic. The mark didn't disappear; the swirl of light just kept pulsing.

He yanked off his shredded clothes and collapsed onto his bed without bothering to shower. His entire body hurt, and the events of the night spun wildly in his thoughts. For a moment, he recalled the diamond's mesmerizing glow, the comforting warmth it radiated before the chaos. *Was it trying to show me something?*

He pulled a blanket over himself, ignoring the grime. Just beyond the edges of sleep, he glimpsed more flickers of that cosmic imagery—visions of star fields and watery worlds. He heard echoes of the hum, too, like a lullaby that made no sense and yet felt oddly soothing.

Eventually, fatigue dragged him under. In the silence of his room, the mark on his palm glowed softly, as if breathing with him. Whatever that cavern had been, it was gone now, sealed behind rubble. But something told Jeremy that this wasn't over—not even close.

Chapter 3

The morning sun streamed through the hallways of Crescent Bay High, bathing the cafeteria in a golden glow. Jeremy leaned back in his plastic chair, tapping the rim of an empty soda can with his fingers. Around him, the usual din of chatter ebbed and flowed—friends talking about weekend plans, freshmen comparing notes for exams, athletes recounting last night's game. He could hear teachers murmuring in the distance, knew they were occasionally casting him disapproving looks, but it was all background noise.

Despite the bustle, Jeremy's focus drifted elsewhere. His mind kept replaying the events of the previous night: the collapsed cavern, the strange machinery embedded in the rock, and that glowing diamond nestled deep underground. Most of all, he couldn't stop thinking about the mark now etched into his palm. He turned his hand over under the table, half expecting it to have vanished. But the faint, circular ripple still pulsed there, synchronized with some invisible rhythm. It wasn't as bright in daylight, yet it remained unmistakably alive on his skin, like a secret he couldn't escape. He clenched his fist, trying to smother a flicker of worry. *What does this mean?*

He'd woken up that morning with bruises from the chase and a dull ache in his ribs, but this was beyond physical pain. His life had flipped upside down in the span of a few hours. Worse still, he had no idea who to turn to. Teachers? He could already imagine their skepticism. He needed someone who could keep an open mind.

He felt adrift, confusion swirling in his chest. His parents would probably freak out. And his surf buddies? Sure, they were beach-smart, but this—this was way beyond their depth. Taking it to the police wasn't an option either. They'd probably just confiscate it … or worse, make him disappear. He needed someone he could trust—someone who could keep a secret and actually knew a thing or two about UFOs.

A movement in the corner of his eye pulled him from his thoughts. He looked up to see Lucas Chu rolling his wheelchair closer to Jeremy's table. Lucas's expression was guarded, uncertain. His tablet rested in his lap, the screen reflecting faint overhead lights. Jeremy realized he hadn't heard him approach—he'd been too caught up in his own head.

"Hey," Lucas said quietly.

Jeremy nodded. "Uh, hey."

They'd never talked much. Lucas was known around school for his obsession with inventing gadgets, scribbling mechanical designs in the library, and occasionally blowing out fuses in the science lab. He was also the kid Darren and his lackeys bullied whenever they got bored—until Jeremy swung a skateboard at Darren's jaw yesterday. That memory made Jeremy smirk for a split second.

Lucas adjusted his grip on the tablet. "I just wanted to say thanks. For what you did yesterday. You didn't have to step in, but … you did."

Jeremy shrugged. "Those guys are jerks. Someone had to do it." He tried to sound dismissive, but a warmth of pride flickered in his chest.

Lucas's lips twitched into a faint smile. "They are jerks. But I'm used to everyone just looking the other way. So it kind of matters. Thanks."

Jeremy nodded, shifting in his seat. It felt odd to be thanked for something he'd done on impulse. He tapped the soda can with renewed focus, the metal clinking softly. "Yeah, well, don't get used to it. Not planning on making hero stuff a habit. Too much work."

Lucas exhaled a tiny laugh. "Fair enough."

A moment of silence passed. Jeremy glanced around the cafeteria—no Darren or Trevor in sight, at least not yet. Slowly, he leaned forward, lowering his voice. "Hey, Lucas … you're into, like, sci-fi and tech, right?"

"Sure," Lucas replied, sounding cautious. "I like all that futuristic stuff. Why?"

Jeremy hesitated. He didn't really know Lucas that well. Could he even be trusted? What if his dad was a cop and ratted him out? Or worse—what if Lucas just wasn't sharp enough and ended up spilling the secret to some random kid who couldn't help him figure any of this out?

And then there was the biggest question of all— how was he supposed to bring up the diamond without sounding completely insane? He decided to go with his gut feeling and tell Lucas.

"I … found something. Something weird. I kind of want a second opinion."

Lucas's eyebrows rose. "Define weird."

Jeremy looked around the cafeteria one more time, making sure nobody eavesdropped. "Not here. Too many people." He grabbed his backpack, slung it over one shoulder, and stood. "C'mon."

They ended up in an empty classroom at the far end of the school. The desks stood in neat rows, the chalkboard dusty with half-erased equations. Sunlight angled through the windows, illuminating tiny flecks of chalk dust in the air. The hum of the air conditioner provided a muted background.

He shut the door behind them, then turned to Lucas. His pulse kicked up a notch. Even now, he questioned whether revealing the diamond was a terrible idea. But something about Lucas's calm curiosity made Jeremy trust him—if only a little.

"Okay," he murmured, setting his backpack on a desk. "Check this out."

He unzipped the bag and gently removed the diamond, placing it on the worn desktop. Its soft, pulsing glow immediately bathed the immediate area in cool bluish-green light. The reflection danced across the classroom walls, turning the stale math space into something ethereal.

Lucas inhaled sharply. "What ... is that?"

"I was hoping you could tell me," Jeremy said. He ran a hand through his hair. "I found it underground. Seriously. I fell through this hole near the school fence when I was trying to escape Darren and them. Down there ... there was this cave with weird metal stuff in the walls. And this ... diamond thing."

Lucas wheeled closer, transfixed by the glow. "No way." His eyes darted over every detail—the diamond's smooth exterior, the gentle flicker of light within. "This is … it's incredible."

"Yeah, it's something," Jeremy mumbled. "But it's also trouble." He turned his palm upward to reveal the faint, glowing ripple, a shudder passing through his spine. Even in the midday light, it pulsed in tandem with the diamond's glow. "Touched it once, and now I'm stuck with this … thing."

Lucas's jaw dropped. "It gave you that mark?"

Jeremy stared at his arm with a mix of awe and dread. "All I know is it won't go away, and every time I look at it, I get this weird feeling. Like there's a connection between me and that rock."

Lucas glanced up, his expression equal parts excitement and concern. "I've never seen anything like this. Are you—did it, I don't know, hurt you? You okay?"

Jeremy let out a humorless chuckle. "I'm alive, if that's what you mean. Just freaked out." He gently tapped the diamond's surface with a fingertip. "Feel how warm it is."

Lucas reached out, brushing the orb with caution. His eyes widened. "It's almost like … your body temperature. That's not normal. A stone this large—" He paused, swallowing. "If it's what I think it is, it's beyond anything we've studied at school."

Jeremy lifted a brow. "You think it's alien or something?"

Lucas looked unsettled. "I … don't know. It's definitely advanced, though. Could be some undiscovered tech. Or an energy source. I won't really know until I can test it."

A flicker of curiosity overcame Jeremy's anxiety. "Test it how?"

Lucas's reply was immediate. "My lab. I have gear there that can analyze samples, run spectrometric scans, that sort of thing." Realizing how that might sound, he added quickly, "It's nothing official, just stuff my dad left behind."

"Your dad?" Jeremy repeated.

"Yeah, he was an engineer. Did some work with the CIA or some intel group before he retired. Left me the workshop—and I upgraded it." Lucas offered a tentative grin. "If you're up for it, I could see what this thing's made of. And maybe figure out what's happening to your hand."

Jeremy glanced at the diamond, at the shimmering swirl of light dancing within it. "Could you really do that?"

Lucas nodded. "I can try. We just have to be careful. If this is dangerous, we need to know right away."

Jeremy exhaled. He was still unsure whether trusting Lucas was wise, but he felt cornered. Who else could possibly help? "All right," he said, picking up the diamond and slipping it back into his bag. "But let's keep this between us, okay? Last thing I need is half the school knowing I've got some glowing rock that could be … alien."

Lucas nodded earnestly. "Deal. Meet me after the last bell, and I'll show you where I live."

***

Crescent Bay High's final bell rang out, releasing a tidal wave of students that flooded the halls. Jeremy took a quick detour to avoid Darren's usual hangouts, then found Lucas waiting at the front entrance. The two boarded a local bus, grabbing seats near the back. The ride was filled with jolting stops and starts, but Jeremy barely noticed. He kept his hand shoved in his hoodie pocket, as if the entire bus might see the glow otherwise.

Lucas's house turned out to be on the outskirts of town. They hopped off the bus at a nearly empty stop, flanked by tall hedges and a winding road. The neighborhood felt quiet, almost eerily so compared to the hustle of downtown Crescent Bay.

"This way," Lucas said, leading Jeremy down a short driveway. The house was modest—single-story with a weathered porch. But in the backyard stood an old, rust-streaked shed. Jeremy would've assumed it was full of gardening tools—until Lucas wheeled up to a hidden keypad behind a loose panel and typed in a sequence of numbers.

A soft beep, and the shed's inner wall slid open with a pneumatic hiss, revealing a secret entrance. Jeremy gawked. "Okay, that's definitely not suspicious at all."

Lucas gave a slight smile. "It's secure. C'mon."

They moved through a dimly lit corridor until it opened into a spacious underground lab, defying the shed's humble exterior. Fluorescent ceiling panels illuminated the scene: shelves stacked with half-built devices, spools of wire, circuit boards, and a variety of high-tech equipment Jeremy couldn't identify. A 3D printer in the corner hummed softly, printing some intricate plastic part. A large workstation dominated the central area, glowing holographic screens hovering above it. And at the far end loomed a tall, cylindrical machine covered in pulsing blue lights.

Jeremy couldn't help but whistle. "Dude ... you built all this?"

Lucas shrugged, maneuvering his wheelchair around a stray coil of tubing. "My dad laid the foundation, but I've been tinkering here for years, modifying, expanding." He paused at the central workstation, spinning one of the holographic panels with a flick of his fingers. "So, let's see that diamond."

Jeremy pulled his backpack off, carefully extracting the glowing orb. In the lab's bright overhead lights, the diamond's pulsing shimmer was more subdued, but still mesmerizing. Lucas rolled closer, his gaze full of wonder.

"This is so amazing." He whistled softly. "You said you found it just sitting in a cave?"

Jeremy nodded. "The cave was full of weird metal stuff—like a crashed ship or something. No clue. I grabbed this before the place collapsed."

Lucas let out a breath, gingerly touching the orb's surface. "Feels ... alive. If it's a power source, it might be generating some low-level field. We can try scanning it with the spectrometer." He opened a drawer under the workstation and pulled out a sleek device shaped like a scanner gun. "This'll give me a basic read on its composition."

He aimed the scanner at the diamond and tapped a button on the holographic console. The device emitted a faint hum, lines of data scrolling across the air in front of them. Jeremy watched the readout, not understanding most of it—percentages, spectral lines, energy wavelengths.

Lucas frowned. "Readings are incomplete," he muttered. "It's not matching any known mineral composition, and the energy output is off the charts. Like it's tapping into something I don't have calibrated."

Jeremy huffed a nervous laugh. "So you're telling me it's alien?"

Lucas hesitated. "I can't say for sure, but I've never seen anything from Earth that behaves like this. It's definitely advanced—and not man-made—as far as I can tell." He set the scanner aside, opening another interface to display a rotating 3D representation of the diamond. The hologram flickered, suggesting the system couldn't capture its full complexity.

"Could it be dangerous?" Jeremy asked quietly.

Lucas glanced from the readout to Jeremy's glowing palm. "Maybe. Or maybe it's a huge opportunity. If we figure out how its energy works, we could replicate clean power, or something even bigger. But yeah, if it's unstable, it could be a problem."

Jeremy swallowed, tension coiling in his gut. "Listen, I just want to know what's happening to me." He held up his hand. "This mark—it lights up anytime I'm near the diamond. It's like they're bonded."

Lucas leaned back, deep in thought. "I might try building a containment module. Something to isolate the diamond's field so it's not in direct contact with you. Then we can observe changes in your palm, see if the mark fades or stays."

Jeremy felt an odd pinch of regret at the idea of sealing the diamond away. He hadn't even realized he'd grown attached to it—though maybe "attached" wasn't the right word. More like he was compelled by it. But the memory of the cavern's collapse, the blasts of debris, reminded him they had to be careful. "Sure. That's a good plan. Let's keep it from blowing up the whole place."

Lucas cracked a small smile. "Exactly." He maneuvered to a side table cluttered with half-built metal containers. "I can probably rig something up to block or dampen its energy signature. Then we can run more tests."

Jeremy nodded, his gaze drifting around the futuristic lab. *How did I end up here?* A day ago, he was just another surfer kid, skipping homework, dodging bullies. Now he stood in a hidden workshop with a classmate he barely knew, researching a glowing orb that might not be from Earth. Despite the anxiety, he felt a surge of excitement. This was ... bigger. Larger than the petty issues at Crescent Bay High. He glanced at Lucas, who was intently measuring a cylindrical container with a digital caliper. "Lucas," he said softly.

Lucas glanced up. "Yeah?"

"Thanks." Jeremy rubbed the back of his neck, trying to find the right words. "I mean, for checking this out. I didn't really know who else to turn to. You're kind of the only person who might ... believe it, you know?"

Lucas's expression softened. "We'll figure it out. Maybe we'll change the world." He patted a metal sheet. "Or we'll blow up half the neighborhood. One of the two."

Jeremy snorted, though the joke held a kernel of real concern. He fished the diamond from the desktop and placed it carefully near Lucas's makeshift parts.

Its glow reflected in Lucas's eyes, making them appear luminescent too.

He didn't know what the future held—whether the diamond was some cosmic battery or an alien artifact. But at least he wasn't facing the mystery alone anymore. For the first time since that terrifying fall into the earth, Jeremy felt a flicker of hope.

Outside, the late-afternoon sun began dipping behind distant rooftops, painting the yard with golden light that trickled through the small windows of the shed. The quiet hum of the lab's machinery underscored the sense that something monumental was unfolding. Jeremy swallowed, reminding himself that even if he didn't have all the answers, he had a clue—and someone willing to help chase it down.

"I'm in," he said, voice steady. "Let's see where this goes."

Lucas nodded, turning back to his workstation. "Then let's get to work."

Chapter 4

Lucas had been obsessively working on *something* for the past two weeks. Barely speaking to Jeremy, he rushed straight to his lab after school each day. In class, he hardly looked up from his sketchbook, constantly scribbling complex diagrams while the teachers droned on—not that he needed to listen. He already knew most of what they were teaching anyway.

Then, out of nowhere, Lucas finally spoke up after school one day. "Hey, man. Sorry I've been so MIA lately. But you *have* to come over tonight. I've got something that will blow your mind."

Curiosity fully piqued, Jeremy showed up that evening, stepping into Lucas's shed-turned-lab. The place was alive—*really* alive. Machines buzzed, wires dangled from the ceiling, and workstations overflowed with half-assembled gadgets. The 3D printer whirred steadily in the corner, building some tiny component layer by layer. Holographic blueprints hovered above the central console, displaying a glowing map of Crescent Bay overlaid with shifting energy patterns.

And then Jeremy saw it.

Laid out across the main worktable was a sleek blue suit, smooth and futuristic, gleaming under the overhead lights. The matching helmet and tinted visor made it look even more like something out of a sci-fi movie.

"What the hell is this?" Jeremy asked, leaning closer. "Dude, did you seriously build some kind of *super suit*? Is this from the diamond? Like, some hidden alien tech or something? This is insane!"

Lucas paused, clearly amused by his reaction. He crossed his arms, eyebrows raised. "Jeremy, my dude. You have *no idea* how insane this actually is." He gestured dramatically to the suit. "The diamond didn't just give me tech—it unlocked possibilities that make quantum computers look like Fisher-Price toys for drooling babies. I'm talking about energy fields, electromagnetic waves, calculations faster than anything on the planet. It's like holding a piece of the universe's source code in your hand. And honestly? I've been at this for two weeks, almost nonstop, and I still feel like I've barely scratched the surface."

Jeremy blinked, his mind struggling to keep up with Lucas's hypercharged explanation. "Uh … cool? So, wait. What does the suit actually *do*? Does it, like … work with the diamond? Iron Man style?"

Lucas scoffed, shaking his head. "No, no, no. Forget your comics for a second. The suit? *My design.* Custom-made. Aerodynamic, wind-resistant, a functional work of art. The helmet? That's just to protect your pretty face when things get … intense."

Before Jeremy could respond, Lucas crouched under the table and pulled out something even wilder.

A surfboard.

But not just any board. It was silver, sleek, and thinner than anything Jeremy had ever seen. It looked futuristic but somehow … elegant, like it had been crafted for speed.

Jeremy's jaw dropped. "No way! What *is* that?"

Lucas grinned, holding the board up like it was the crown jewel of his work. "This, my friend, is where things get *really* crazy. Check this out."

He turned to his console and tapped a few keys. The holographic map shifted, zooming in on Crescent Bay. Strange, glowing lines rippled across the landscape.

"See these waves?" Lucas pointed at the grid overlaying the map.

Jeremy nodded, eyes wide.

"Using your diamond's energy, I hacked into the global satellite network and created a wave grid—an invisible energy pattern that can project *anywhere* on Earth. In other words, you're not limited to the ocean anymore, bro. Every building, every street, every hill— they're all waves now. You can ride them. *Literally.*"

Jeremy staggered back, running both hands through his hair. "No. No way. You're saying … I could surf the *entire world*? Like, every time I've seen a hill and thought, 'Man, I wish that was a wave,' you're telling me I can actually *do* that now?"

Lucas just nodded, a smug grin plastered on his face.

"Dude, this is—this is the sickest thing I've ever seen! Are you messing with me? Is there a hidden camera somewhere? Because this is unreal!"

He practically tackled Lucas in a hug, jumping around like a kid on Christmas morning.

But then, just as the excitement peaked, reality hit him. He stopped cold.

"Wait, bro. How do I even test this? What if I fall? This whole thing looks insane—and kinda terrifying, not gonna lie."

Lucas chuckled, leaning casually against the table. "Chill, man. First off, the wave grid? Only *you* can see it, so it'll guide you. Second, the suit helps you stay on the grid—even if you wipe out, you won't just drop like a rock. But listen ..." He grew serious for a moment. "It has limits. If you fall from too high or push it too hard, it might not hold you perfectly. And this? This isn't the ocean, dude. Riding energy grids? It's a whole new ball game."

Jeremy stared at the suit and board, heart pounding. The possibilities raced through his mind.

This wasn't just surfing.

It was the future.

And he *had* to try it.

Slipping into the suit felt like sliding on a second skin. It clung snugly without constricting his movement, its panels stitched with luminous lines that faintly glowed a soft electric blue. The helmet fit comfortably over his head, the visor tinted dark enough to hide his features. He gave a tentative wave in front of his face. Through the visor's interface, he glimpsed a crisp display of the lab, overlain with subtle data readouts.

Lucas rolled over, holding out the board. "Let's give it a go, my friend."

Jeremy propped the board under his arm. "Yeah, I guess this is going to feel very different. I will just need to let the wave guide me and try to go with the flow."

"Exactly." Lucas whirled back to his console, tapping a final sequence. A holographic map of the city brightened. "I'm feeding the wave projection from the satellites. Once you're outside, your visor will reveal the grid. And no one else can see it."

Jeremy allowed himself a grin. "Time to show Crescent Bay something new."

They decided to begin at dusk, so the city lights would create a dramatic backdrop—but also because the presence of fewer cars on the roads would reduce the risk of any collisions.

Jeremy stepped out into a back alley behind the lab. The moment he put on the visor, a network of rippling lines shimmered across the pavement.

"Everything's stable on my end," Lucas said through the suit's built-in audio link. "You're good to go."

Jeremy set the board on the ground and stepped on. He shifted his weight, leaning forward. Instantly, the board rose a few inches off the asphalt, buoyed by an invisible wave. A rush of excitement shot through him.

"Time to take this baby on the road," he murmured, pressing gently into the wave. He glided down the alley, the suit's luminous lines a faint glow in the evening's dim light.

When he emerged onto a wider street, he braced himself for the city's reaction. Cars meandered along, and a few pedestrians wandered the sidewalk. None of them noticed him at first—he was just a figure among the shadows. Then a streetlamp illuminated him fully, revealing the blue suit and the board hovering above the pavement.

"Look!" gasped a teenager waiting at a crosswalk. "What is that?"

Jeremy grinned behind the visor. "Let's give them a show."

He leaned forward more boldly, and the board shot down the street. Air whipped past him. The wave lines, visible only in his visor, rose and fell gently, letting him carve around parked cars and weave between lampposts. Heads turned, and a growing chorus of surprise spread among the onlookers.

"Is he ... surfing?" someone shouted.

A car horn blared as a stunned driver slowed to watch Jeremy swoop overhead. He soared up a gentle wave that arced two or three feet above the pavement, clearing the car's hood. The driver's face, half hanging out the window, twisted into sheer disbelief.

"This is insane," Jeremy muttered under his breath, heart racing, but in a good way—like catching the perfect wave in the ocean, except the "ocean" was now Crescent Bay's streets.

As he navigated onto a busier avenue, the reaction intensified. People on sidewalks paused mid-step, their phones snapping up to record. A group of teens at a corner store spilled out, dropping sodas as they witnessed the blue-suited figure gliding by. One kid yelled, "Yo, that's the coolest thing I've ever seen!"

A convertible full of teenagers screeched to a halt, its passengers leaning out and screaming in excitement, cameras flashing. "You see that?" one of them yelled, voice crackling with adrenaline. "Is that one of those attack drones? Maybe it's an alien!"

Jeremy felt pure exhilaration. He bent his knees, carving around a city bus that slammed on its brakes, the driver's jaw practically on the steering wheel. Some of the passengers pressed their faces against the windows, eyes wide.

"This is unreal," Jeremy said. He heard Lucas chuckle through the earpiece.

"Sure is. You're blowing up social media right now," Lucas said. "But your visor's dark enough that no one can see your face, so you're in the clear."

Perfect. Jeremy banked hard around a corner, the wave lines reconfiguring in his visor. Buildings loomed ahead, and a ripple in the grid angled sharply upward. He crouched low, leaning into the momentum. In a heartbeat, he soared up the side of a short building, landing on its rooftop in a smooth glide.

Pigeons scattered, flapping in panic. Jeremy let out a startled laugh. "Sorry, guys!"

He cruised along the rooftop's invisible wave, the city's lights twinkling below. It was a breathtaking view—rows of streetlights, neon signs, and passing cars. A family in an apartment across the way gaped through their window as he glided past. One man nearly dropped his coffee mug.

"Hi," Jeremy murmured, bemused. The man's eyes bulged, and Jeremy couldn't help but grin.

Easing off the rooftop, he soared back into open air. The wave lines carried him across an intersection, prompting more honks and exclamations from startled drivers. A small child on the sidewalk pointed up, eyes shining. "Mommy, look! A superhero!"

A strange warmth filled Jeremy's chest. He wasn't exactly a superhero, but he certainly looked the part tonight—an anonymous figure in glimmering blue. He swerved between lampposts, the board responding fluidly with every tilt of his hips.

"Hey, Jeremy." Lucas's voice crackled in his ear. "You see that big suspension bridge up ahead, right?"

Jeremy glanced toward the horizon. The city's main bridge arched over the water, lit by a series of lamps that made its cables glow. Through his visor, he could see wave lines climbing the steel supports. He swallowed. "Yeah, I see it."

"Think you can handle it?"

"Only one way to find out."

He glided down a major boulevard, weaving around cars. People on motorbikes nearly crashed, trying to get a glimpse of him. The entire city seemed mesmerized. As he approached the bridge, the wave lines rose high, guiding him to the first set of cables. He bent his knees, bracing himself.

A moment later, he was surfing the bridge's steel cables, the whole structure humming in the night air. The water below reflected the city lights, and the top of the bridge gave him a panoramic view of Crescent Bay. He exhaled in awe. The warm breeze carried the sounds of distant traffic and clanging buoy bells from the harbor.

On the lower decks, drivers stared upward. One passenger leaned halfway out of a car window, pointing in disbelief. A group of tourists on foot shrieked with excitement. Through the earpiece, Lucas's voice came again. "You're literally surfing a bridge, my friend. How does it feel?"

Jeremy couldn't suppress a laugh. "Feels like I'm on top of the world!"

He let the wave guide him up one cable, across the central arch, and then down the other side. The smooth gliding sensation reminded him of catching a perfect wave back at the beach—except this was infinitely larger and far more surreal. The cityscape sprawled out before him, a luminous tapestry in the dark.

Descending from the bridge, Jeremy swooped back into the urban sprawl. Horns blared, pedestrians shouted, and phone screens glowed everywhere. A young couple walking their dog froze mid-step, jaws dropping. "Is he f-f-flying?" the woman stammered.

"Looks like it!" the man replied, fumbling for his phone.

A bike courier nearly toppled over as Jeremy swept past, leaving a ripple of excitement in his wake. Laughter bubbled in Jeremy's chest. The freedom of it all was intoxicating—no fear of recognition, no worrying about tomorrow. Just the thrill of surfing the city under the stars.

He soared over a parked convertible where a group of friends hollered and filmed him. "This is going viral, dude!" one screamed.

"Watch out, man, he might be an alien! We should get the army down here now!" another shouted nervously.

Jeremy flashed a quick thumbs-up, though he doubted they could see the wink behind his tinted visor. Still, hearing their giddy reactions made him grin.

Continuing on, he hopped onto a low-rise building, then leaped to a taller one when the wave lines provided a rising crest. On each rooftop, the city lights shimmered around him, painting the sky with neon pinks and blues. A restaurant's open-air terrace erupted in cheers as patrons spotted him gliding past. One guy actually stood on his chair, pointing. "Look at that, look at that!"

Jeremy shot him a friendly wave, then curved off the rooftop's edge back into the open air. He'd never imagined something like this could exist, even in his wildest daydreams; surfing the city, in total anonymity, with nothing but the hush of the wind and the scattered oohs and aahs of onlookers.

As he skimmed across a busy intersection, a car screeched to a halt. The driver stuck their head out, shouting, "Did you see that?!" Meanwhile, a group of skateboarders at a plaza lost their minds, whooping in collective amazement.

A street performer strumming a guitar paused mid-chord to stare. The half dozen people watching the performance redirected their attention to Jeremy overhead. Cameras flashed like lightning strikes. A kid dropped his ice cream cone, eyes so wide it was comical.

Lucas's voice chimed in his ear. "Jeremy, you're basically the talk of the town right now. People are tagging #CitySurfer, #BlueSurfer, #AirSurf. It's trending like crazy."

Jeremy laughed, adjusting his stance to arc around a tall sculpture in the center of a traffic roundabout. "This is the coolest feeling ever," he said. "No pressure, no fear. Just living it up."

He decided to wrap up his ride in a large public park near the bay. The wave lines guided him downward, drifting across a grassy field where families picnicked under paper lanterns. The onlookers gasped and stood up, pointing at the blue figure floating by.

A small cluster of kids sprinted in his direction, shouting, "Wait, come back!"

He gave them a playful grin, though they only saw a mirrored visor.

Near the edge of the park, he glided to a stop. The board gently settled onto the ground. For a split second, the entire park seemed to hold its breath. Then applause and cheers erupted, echoing off nearby trees.

Jeremy turned, hopped back on the board, and nudged forward. A final wave carried him behind a grove of tall bushes, out of sight. By the time the crowd had hurried over to see if he'd vanished, he was already slipping down a side path, drifting away in silence.

After a few more blocks, Jeremy ducked into a quiet alley, stepped off the board, and tucked it under his arm. The wave grid in his visor showed a safe route back to Lucas's secret entrance. He followed the outlines, hugging shadowy back lanes until he reached the unmarked door leading into the lab.

Inside, he pulled off the helmet, letting out a deep breath. Lucas was at the console, a grin plastered across his face. "Dude, that was incredible. I have like thirty different live streams going here. No one has a clue who you are. Just 'the surfer in blue.'"

Jeremy peeled off the top half of the suit, wiping sweat from his brow. "It felt like I was on one endless wave. I must've gone all over the city."

"You did. Social media's lighting up. Everyone's talking about the 'mystery surfer' showing off in the sky."

Jeremy laughed, euphoria still buzzing in his veins. He grabbed a bottle of water from a mini-fridge, gulping it down. "I kind of can't believe it myself. Surfing rooftops, bridging traffic, making kids drop their ice cream? Best day ever!"

Lucas pivoted his chair, eyes gleaming. "This is a sick ride, isn't it?"

"Oh yes," Jeremy said firmly.

If he was honest, he felt a tiny pang of curiosity about tomorrow—would the city try to figure out who he was? But for now, that didn't matter. Thanks to the tinted visor and the hidden wave grid, he was safe, free, and riding a high he never knew existed.

Lucas raised a fist, and Jeremy bumped it. "This is just the start," Lucas said, a mischievous spark in his eyes. "Imagine what else we can do once we refine everything."

A grin tugged at Jeremy's lips. "I'm in. Let's keep the waves rolling."

They shared a satisfied laugh, both marveling at how quickly their lives had transformed. A couple of weeks ago, Jeremy was just a surfer kid dodging school obligations, and Lucas was an under-the-radar genius tinkering alone. Now, they were partners in an extraordinary new pastime—urban surfing on invisible waves.

The satellites overhead followed Lucas's coded commands, shaping intangible swells for Jeremy to ride. And out there, across Crescent Bay, countless people were likely still recounting the insane spectacle they'd witnessed.

But for Jeremy, the night's excitement was enough. He peeled away the rest of the suit, changed into fresh clothes, and flopped onto an old couch in the corner. Grinning to himself, he let his mind replay the best moments—the bridge, the rooftops, the cheers.

Even though the city might be abuzz, he felt only anticipation for the next ride.

He and Lucas had tapped into something magical, and they were just getting started. Whatever else happened tomorrow, he'd never forget the feeling of cutting across the sky, the wave beneath his feet, the wind on his helmet, and the city cheering below him. This was real freedom.

And he craved more.

Chapter 5

The lab hummed softly with the whirr of cooling fans and the intermittent crackle of wiring. Monitors flickered against the walls, their luminescent glow mingling with the pulsing blue light emanating from the diamond perched on the workstation. The scene was equal parts high-tech haven and improvised workshop: cables snaked across the floor, half-built devices piled on every flat surface, and holographic schematics hovered midair, displaying data that Jeremy barely understood.

He sat in a metal-backed chair against one wall, lazily spinning his surfboard upright by its rail. His expression was distant, as though his mind were somewhere else entirely. Lucas, on the other hand, looked thoroughly absorbed in his element—wheeling between one workstation and another, tapping commands on glowing consoles. Every now and then, he mumbled to himself in that hyper-focused way of his.

Finally, Lucas spun around, practically bouncing in his seat. "Okay," he said, voice brimming with excitement. "We've tested the wave grid a bunch of times now. You have the suit, the board, and you've proven you can handle the city-surfing. I'd say it's time for the next step."

Jeremy paused the spin of his surfboard. "Next step?"

Lucas nodded eagerly. "Becoming a hero."

Jeremy exhaled through his nose, half a laugh, half annoyance. "A hero? What the hell are you talking about?"

"I'm serious," Lucas insisted, rolling his chair closer so that stray wires and screws scattered under his wheels. "Think about it. You can ride the wave grids over the entire city in seconds. You're practically flying. That means you can show up where people need help— robberies, fires, whatever. You'd be unstoppable."

Jeremy set the surfboard tip-down on the floor, glancing up at him. "No one's unstoppable, especially not me."

Lucas waved him off. "You know what I mean. You have a huge advantage. You could be a symbol for hope. Someone who saves the day—like a superhero. Why not use these abilities for something bigger than yourself? Besides, I am also taking a huge risk here, you know. I'm hacking all kinds of computers and ordering all this weird stuff online so I can improve the grid and the suit. I'm pretty sure I'm picking some vibes from my old man, but he doesn't know what we are doing, at least not yet."

"I just wanted to surf," Jeremy said, leaning back against the wall. His tone turned defensive. "I didn't ask to become some vigilante or a do-gooder. I'm sixteen, Lucas. School's enough of a headache."

Lucas threw up his hands. "But you already are doing more than a normal sixteen-year-old. You're basically defying gravity with a high-tech board. Why not help people while you're at it?"

"Because," Jeremy began, irritation lacing his voice, "I didn't choose any of this. The diamond, the satellites, the wave grids … It's all bigger than I asked for. I'm not interested in police scanners and saving puppies from burning buildings. I just want to carve some air-waves and not get grounded for ditching homework."

Lucas's enthusiasm faded, replaced by frustration. "You're wasting your gifts if you don't at least consider it. People out there need help every day, and you're too busy being too cool to care."

"Wasting it, huh?" Jeremy bristled, standing up and grabbing his surfboard under one arm. "So I'm a bad person because I don't want your superhero fantasies?"

"I didn't say you're bad. Just … self-centered," Lucas shot back. "You can do so much good. Why won't you see that?"

Jeremy's face darkened, anger sparking behind his eyes. "Maybe I don't care about being some noble icon, all right? Not everyone wants to be a big freaking hero."

They locked eyes, the crackling tension in the air almost visible. For a moment, the lab's hum was the only sound.

Then Jeremy spun on his heel, surfboard clutched tightly. "Call me when you come up with something fun," he said coldly. "Otherwise, I'm out."

Lucas didn't argue; he just stared at Jeremy's retreating figure as the lab door slammed shut behind him.

***

Jeremy was still fuming by the time he'd walked the few blocks to his house, tucked in a quiet residential neighborhood. The argument with Lucas replayed on loop in his head, stoking his frustration. *Why can't he just accept that I'm not cut out for hero stuff?* he thought.

But all that anger evaporated the second he opened his front door. Tension choked the air inside, heavier than any fight with Lucas. His mother paced by the window, phone clutched in her trembling hands, while his father stood stiffly by the couch, face drawn and worried.

"What's going on?" Jeremy blurted, heart picking up speed.

His mom turned, her eyes red. "Maddison ... She was on a school trip. Kayaking. She—she fell off her boat, and they can't find her."

Jeremy's gut twisted. "What? Can't find her—where? How?"

His dad's voice was low and shaky. "They're searching the river, but daylight's fading, and the current's too strong. No one's seen her for hours."

A surge of pure dread gripped Jeremy. Maddison. His little sister—the kid who adored him, who tried to mimic his surf moves on her boogie board—lost in a dangerous river? He didn't wait for more details. He spun on his heel and bolted out the door, ignoring his mom's startled calls. He had to do something.

A short sprint later, Jeremy burst back into Lucas's lab, breath ragged. Whatever tension or bitterness he'd felt earlier no longer mattered. "Lucas!" he shouted, voice cracking with urgency. "I need your help. Maddison's missing on a river. She fell off a kayak, they can't find her. Please."

Lucas's eyes widened, the earlier argument forgotten. "Where did this happen?"

Jeremy sputtered the location, explaining it was several miles from Crescent Bay, in a forested region with fast rapids. "You said the diamond's frequencies can track living things or something? Or maybe the satellites can show you anomalies on the wave grid? I don't care if it's half-baked, just help me find her!"

Lucas nodded, rolling to his main console. "I'll do what I can." He launched a quick interface, linking the diamond's scanning feature to his newly developed wave-projection software. Graphs and a topographic map flickered on-screen. "I can't promise perfection, but maybe we can get a reading of any large heat signatures near the river. Or pick up something from her phone, if it's still functioning."

Seconds felt like hours as Jeremy paced. Finally, Lucas froze, pointing at a faint blip near a bend in the river. "There! I'm getting some sign of a person near the water. Could be her. Coordinates locked."

"Thanks." Jeremy grabbed the blue wave-surfing suit, stepping into it. Normally, he would complain or roll his eyes at playing "city surfer," but now he was desperate. "I'll bring her straight home," he said, voice quivering. "No time to lose."

With a quick nod from Lucas, Jeremy activated the wave grid in his visor. The lines spread out across the city, connecting to the satellites overhead. With a surge of speed, he soared out of the lab, weaving between rooftops until he was free of the urban sprawl. The sun was sinking, painting the sky in oranges and pinks. Jeremy pushed the board to its limit, heart thudding in his chest. *Hold on, Maddison. I'm coming.*

Soon, the grid guided him over swaths of forest, where thick trees cast looming shadows in the twilight. His visor scanned the terrain below—rocky riverbanks, swirling rapids. Sweat beaded on Jeremy's forehead, partly from the intense concentration and partly from fear.

Lightning flickered in the distance, heralding an approaching storm. The wind gusted, threatening to tear him off course. Still, he pressed on, the wave lines adjusting for the uneven ground below. At last, he spotted a bright-orange kayak pinned against some rocks. A smaller shape clung to a slick boulder near the middle of the raging river—Maddison, her arms wrapped around it, eyes wide with terror.

"Maddison!" Jeremy shouted, though she couldn't hear him over the roar. His stomach knotted at the sight of the river's fierce current. Without hesitation, he dove closer, aiming for the narrow gap between jagged rocks.

Rain began spattering the canopy overhead. Another flash of lightning revealed a heart-stopping detail on the shore: a large black bear prowled near the riverbank, drawn by the commotion or maybe the scent of fear.

No time for that now—gotta get my sister!

Jeremy dipped the board low, leaning forward so he nearly skimmed the water's surface. Maddison gasped, startled by the sudden appearance of a blue-suited figure gliding above the rapids.

The current slammed over the rocks, nearly washing her away. Jeremy swooped in, extending his hand. She let out a cry but then latched onto his forearm. In one swift motion, he hauled her onto the narrow board behind him. The board shuddered under the weight; he gritted his teeth, forcing it upward, away from the water's deadly pull. The black bear snarled onshore as if in protest, but Jeremy and Maddison soared above the treetops, carried by an invisible wave.

Breathing hard, Jeremy angled the board back toward Crescent Bay. The storm rumbled, scattering droplets across his visor. Maddison clung to him, soaked and trembling, tears blending with the rain on her face. She didn't speak, too shocked to process the rescue just yet.

They flew over the outskirts of town. Streetlights winked on in the dusk, and a few passing cars slowed, their drivers craning their necks at the surreal sight of two figures on a floating board. Jeremy ignored it all— he had one goal: bring Maddison home safe.

A minute later, he descended onto his own front lawn, the board touching down gently on the grass. Stunned neighbors stepped onto their porches to see what was going on. Jeremy quickly helped Maddison onto solid ground. She wobbled, nearly collapsing from exhaustion.

Their parents burst through the front door, disbelief and relief mingling on their faces. "Maddison!" their mom cried, rushing forward. Their dad followed, speechless but clearly overjoyed. Maddison stumbled into their arms, soaked but alive.

Jeremy remained on the board, wearing the visor that concealed his face. For a split second, he thought about removing it, but decided to leave it on. He did not want his parents to know he was the sky surfer;

deep inside, he felt that this story with the diamond and the suit might unfold to unexpected places, and he wanted to keep his family on the safe side.

"Is she okay?" he asked in a muffled voice.

His mom blinked, tears streaming. "She—yes, but who ...? How ...?"

Jeremy glanced at Maddison, who stared back, dazed. He didn't want her to panic or blow his cover. So he simply murmured, "I'm just glad she's safe," and turned toward the yard's edge. Before anyone could protest, he leaped onto the board and launched back into the air, quickly disappearing over the rooftops. Gasps and exclamations trailed behind him.

***

Back in the lab, the adrenaline was still pounding in Jeremy's veins when he tore off the helmet and suit.

Lucas spun around in his chair. "You did it!"

Jeremy slumped onto a nearby stool, heart still hammering. "Yeah," he panted. "She's home, safe. My parents were freaking out, neighbors gawking ... No one recognized me."

Lucas let out a relieved breath. "Good. I was afraid you might expose yourself. This could have been a disaster."

For a moment, Jeremy rubbed his eyes, recalling the raw panic on Maddison's face and the rush of saving her at the last second. Then he gave a quiet laugh, part exhaustion, part something else. "If it weren't for your tracking system and the wave grid ... she might not be alive."

Lucas's expression turned gentle. "I'm just glad we got her back."

Jeremy swallowed hard. "You know, I have been pushing back hard on this hero stuff. I'm just a surfer …" He trailed off, blinking away lingering raindrops. "But now it feels different."

Lucas nodded, letting him find the words.

A tremor of emotion flickered in Jeremy's eyes. "I wanted to surf the city for the thrill—but this is something bigger. Saving Maddison, seeing my parents so grateful … If there are others who need help, maybe I can do it. Not because I want fame or anything, but because it's the right thing."

Lucas smiled. "So, you're open to the hero idea now?"

Jeremy shook his head, almost amused. "Let's just say I'm not dismissing it. But I'm not plastering my face on TV or wearing a cape. I still want to keep things low-key."

Lucas raised both hands in a mock surrender. "No cape—got it. Just do what you do best and help folks when you can."

Jeremy exhaled slowly, relief washing over him. "I guess we can figure it out as we go. One step at a time."

Lucas grinned. "We're a team—like I said—a dynamic duo. You on the front lines, me on the tech side. We'll keep it chill."

Jeremy managed a small, genuine smile. The terror and anger of earlier melted away, replaced by a sense of purpose. He glanced at the diamond in its cradle, still glowing softly, then back at the door he'd just come through. "Thanks, Lucas. For everything."

Lucas waved off the gratitude. "I only turned on some satellites. You did the brave part."

Jeremy yawned, the adrenaline fading and exhaustion setting in. "I'm heading home. I've got to check on Maddison, see if she's okay enough to talk. Probably do some damage control with my parents."

Lucas nodded. "See you tomorrow, man. And hey—good job."

Jeremy flashed a tired grin. "Thanks." He grabbed his old-school skateboard from the corner—his disguise for the final block home—and left the lab, heart lighter than before. The night air felt calmer, the storm drifting away beyond the city's skyline.

By the time he slipped into his house again, the front lawn was empty, the neighbors having retreated indoors. Maddison was wrapped in blankets on the couch, sipping warm tea while his parents fussed over her. She looked up as Jeremy entered, eyes misty.

"Jer," she whispered. "You won't believe what happened. Some … some guy in a suit flew me home."

He feigned a look of astonishment. "Flew you home? That's wild! I'm just glad you're all right."

She smiled weakly, relief shining through her fatigue. Their parents huddled closer, overjoyed just to have Maddison safe. Jeremy stepped aside to let them coddle her, quietly grateful that no one suspected his secret role in her rescue.

Before going to his room, he offered Maddison a gentle fist bump. She returned it, a tiny spark in her tired eyes. With that, he trudged upstairs, every muscle sore from the tension of the night. He flopped onto his bed, staring at the dark ceiling.

In his mind's eye, he saw the swirl of city lights, the wave lines, and his sister's frightened face. He could practically still hear Lucas's voice over the headset, guiding him through the storm. Slowly, a calm settled over him—a realization that he could do real good with these powers. He might not want to be a poster-boy hero, but if people needed him, he'd be there.

The next day would bring questions, news coverage, and rumors about a mysterious surfer who swooped in to save a girl from the wilderness. For now, though, Jeremy let himself drift into a deep, exhausted sleep. He was only sixteen, still a high school student, still in over his head. But tonight, at least, he'd done something that truly mattered—and that feeling made him certain life would never be the same again.

Chapter 6

The city at night was a living canvas. Neon lights splashed color onto wet pavement, while voices, horns, and distant music intertwined in a restless urban soundtrack. From his vantage point atop a high-rise, Jeremy watched the traffic creep along glistening streets, headlights glowing like lanterns in the dark. The wind tugged at him, carrying hints of rain and distant sea breezes, reminding him of the ocean waves he used to chase.

He tapped the side of his goggles, activating the grid overlay. Instantly, the cityscape took on another dimension: a series of intangible waves rolling across rooftops, alleyways, and signage. Only he could see these fluctuating lines of energy, courtesy of the hacked satellites that Lucas had configured. It was Jeremy's personal ocean in the sky, letting him surf above the hustle of Crescent Bay as though he were on a perfect swell.

"Hey, surfer boy," crackled Lucas's voice through Jeremy's earpiece, slicing through his thoughts. "You planning to do anything tonight, or just daydream?"

Jeremy smirked. "Gimme a sec. Always waiting on you to feed me some intel."

Lucas snorted. "Oh, I've got plenty. According to the scanner, we've got a mugger with a stolen purse a few blocks north. Wanna go break some hearts?"

Jeremy glanced at the shimmering expanse of the city. "Give me the location."

Lucas rattled off a nearby intersection. "Police call says the suspect's heading into an alley."

"On it," Jeremy said, shifting his weight. The hoverboard beneath him responded smoothly, gliding forward. He leaned in, feeling the adrenaline spike as the wind whipped past.

Two seconds later, he dove off the rooftop and soared over a bustling avenue. Curious faces and a few camera phones tilted upward from the sidewalks, but he shot by too fast to be more than a blur. The grid lines drew him onward, weaving between buildings in a graceful arc. Somewhere below, honking cars and night revelers went about their routines, oblivious to the near-silent flight overhead.

"All right," Lucas advised through the comms, "he's cutting through a narrow passage. Swing left at the next block."

Jeremy dropped low, skimming just above the pavement as he entered the alley. Light from distant streetlamps barely penetrated this dark corridor, but he easily spotted the suspect: a wiry man in a black hoodie clutching a purse, eyes darting around. The moment he saw Jeremy—silhouetted by the faint glow of his gear—he let out a startled expletive.

"What the—?!"

Jeremy didn't respond. He crouched, slanting the board sideways to block the alley's exit. Panicked, the mugger tried to double back, only to slip on garbage strewn across the alley floor. He sprawled to the ground in a heap of curses.

Jeremy eased to a stop. He hopped off his board, letting it hover a foot above the concrete. "Hey, man," he said flatly, "pretty sure that's not your purse."

Looking rattled, the mugger shoved the purse forward. "Fine! Take it! I didn't want any trouble."

Jeremy grabbed it, then flipped his wrist. The grid shimmered, momentarily suspending the purse in midair. A small drone—a discreet contraption Lucas had built—whizzed through the alley, grabbed the bag, and zoomed out into the night.

"Delivery complete," Lucas said in Jeremy's ear. "You guys make a cute pair."

Jeremy rolled his eyes. "Just being efficient," he muttered. Turning to the mugger, he added, "No more stealing. People work hard for their stuff."

The man just stared, speechless, as Jeremy stepped back onto his board. A gentle tilt forward, and he rose into the air. Within seconds, he was gone, the hoverboard propelling him above the rooftops. His earpiece crackled with Lucas's laughter.

***

Jeremy's life took on a new rhythm. By day, he was a regular sixteen-year-old grappling with homework, teachers, and the general chaos of high school. But when night fell, the city became his playground. From Lucas's tech-laden lab, police scanners and social media feeds funneled real-time alerts into Jeremy's headset, directing him to small crises: a stolen phone, a hit-and-run suspect, a break-in at a bodega.

He enjoyed helping people—occasionally returning a lost pet to a tearful owner or retrieving a wallet for someone who thought they'd never see it again. The more dramatic nights found him halting brawls before they spiraled out of control or intercepting petty criminals in the midst of break-ins. Regardless of the scale, each act earned him a growing legend among Crescent Bay's night owls.

Social media exploded with shaky videos and half-coherent eyewitness accounts. A strange figure on a futuristic board soared between rooftops, retrieving stolen items or breaking up fights before speeding away. People offered a variety of nicknames, from "Wave Rider" to "Surfing Savior" or "City Surfer." Hashtags abounded: #WaveRiderSaves, #MysterySurfer, #SurfHero. Local news anchors debated whether this was some new vigilante or simply a well-meaning Good Samaritan with advanced tech.

"It's so weird to see your face on these compilations," Lucas noted one evening, spinning in his work chair and playing a fan-made video. Montage clips of Jeremy gliding over the skyline were set to triumphant music. "Well, not your face exactly, but your ... you-ness."

"Kind of freaky," Jeremy admitted, arms crossed. "It's all so public. But I guess as long as I don't get recognized in real life, it's okay."

"Stay anonymous and you'll be fine," Lucas agreed. "But you've got style, man. That alone sets you above most costumed heroes."

Jeremy snorted. "Could do without the public hype. I'm just returning lost dogs or stopping random fights. It's not like I'm changing the world."

Lucas smirked. "Every little act matters, Jer. Don't sell yourself short."

***

Late on a Friday, Crescent Bay's downtown bustled with weekend revelers and neon glow. Jeremy, perched on a ledge above the waterfront, let the city's heartbeat wash over him. He found a strange serenity in these high vantage points, a sense that everything below was part of an interconnected dance.

Lucas's voice broke the spell. "Jeremy, you gotta hear this. It's not a standard police call—someone's streaming live from a diner on Fifth Street. A girl's in trouble. She looks beat-up and terrified, crying for help. The feed's not widely viewed, but it's definitely happening now."

Jeremy tensed, pressing a finger to his earpiece. "No one called the cops?"

"Doesn't sound like it. Or at least, it hasn't reached the scanner. You better check it out before it's too late."

Jeremy sprang onto his board. "Send me the location."

A blinking beacon appeared in his visor. He dove off the ledge, threading through the sky with fluid movements. Street by street, the illusions of wave lines guided his path until he spotted a dingy diner whose neon sign flickered uncertainly. It sat on a run-down block, windows grimy, the sidewalk lonely under a sputtering streetlamp.

Jeremy touched down on the roof, crouching near a skylight. He peered inside and felt his stomach twist. A teenage girl leaned against a booth, trembling, her face bruised. A heavyset man in a stained apron towered over her, voice a harsh, slurred bark.

"You think you can just leave when you want?" he roared, grabbing her wrist. "You're nothing, you hear? You do as I say!"

The girl bit back a sob, fear etched on her features.

"Lucas," Jeremy whispered, anger burning in his chest, "she's not just in trouble. She's trapped."

Lucas's reply was subdued. "I'm guessing forced labor or trafficking. Get her out of there. Fast."

Jeremy slipped off the roof and stepped in through the diner's front entrance, triggering the bell above the door. The man spun, releasing the girl's wrist. His bloodshot eyes narrowed at the sight of Jeremy.

"You lost, kid? This is a private establishment."

Jeremy advanced, letting the door swing shut behind him. "She's leaving with me."

The man snorted, reeking of booze and aggression. "Oh, is that so? How about you get out before I teach you a lesson, too?"

The girl cast Jeremy a desperate look, tears glistening on her cheeks. He met her gaze briefly, hoping to convey reassurance. Then he fixed his attention on the man, mind racing. No time for subtlety.

"She's done here," Jeremy said flatly. "Let her go, and no one gets hurt."

The man sneered, raising a hand as if to strike. Jeremy lunged, blocking the blow and twisting the man's arm just enough to force him back. The older man let out a strangled yelp.

"Don't," Jeremy warned, voice taut. "Leave her alone."

He gestured at the girl. "Go," he said gently. "Now!"

Fear and relief flooded her eyes. With a shaky nod, she bolted past them, pushing open the diner door and fleeing into the night.

The man tried to break free from Jeremy's grip, cursing up a storm. "You messed with the wrong people," he snarled. "She's got no papers! The cops won't protect her. She's mine."

Jeremy's gut twisted in disgust. "Not anymore." He shoved the man backward, grabbed his board, and stepped outside. Before the man could follow, Jeremy powered into the air, ascending in a rush of wind that left the diner behind.

"Lucas," Jeremy said, scanning the nearby streets from above. "She took off. You see her?"

Lucas paused, presumably checking cameras or social media. "Yeah—about a block away, in an alley. She looks terrified."

Jeremy zoomed low over rooftops, then spotted the silhouette of a small figure huddled near a trash bin. He landed softly in the alley, the hoverboard's hum receding. The girl flinched, spinning around in alarm, but recognized him a beat later.

"Are … are you him?" she stammered, eyes darting to his suit, which still faintly shimmered with the wave grid's energy.

He nodded, voice gentle. "Yeah. My name's Jeremy. Are you okay?"

She shook her head, tears brimming again. "He'll find me. I have nowhere to go. Please, don't let him—"

Jeremy stepped closer, raising a calming hand. "You're safe now. I'm not gonna let him hurt you. But that guy obviously has power over you. We need to get you somewhere he can't reach. Will you trust me?"

She hesitated, hugging her arms. "I don't have a choice."

Jeremy lowered his board, gesturing for her to climb on. "We'll go to a lab—a friend's place. We'll figure out what to do from there."

The girl, trembling, nodded. She climbed onto the board behind him, arms wrapped tight around his waist. Jeremy engaged the grid, lifting them above the alley. She gasped, clinging to him as they soared over the dark streets.

The door to Lucas's domain slid open with a pneumatic hiss. The girl—still shaking—followed Jeremy inside. The lab was a chaotic jumble of wires, half-built hardware, and flickering screens. Lucas was at the central console, eyes glued to the monitors. He spun around in his chair, gaze flicking from Jeremy to the frightened newcomer.

"Did you get away clean?" he asked Jeremy, brow furrowed.

Jeremy nodded, guiding the girl to a corner chair. "We're okay. But it's bad, Lucas. That guy was basically holding her hostage."

She sank into the seat, pressing trembling fingers to her forehead. "My name is Sophia," she said softly. "I'm not here legally. He … he brought me here with promises of a better life. My father paid them all he had, but now they use me for forced labor. If I try to leave, they threaten me."

Jeremy's hands curled into fists. "So it's human trafficking."

Lucas grimaced at his screens. "I tapped into the diner owner's background. He's got ties to a bigger network—Russian mob types, known for smuggling undocumented people and forcing them into exploitative jobs." He paused, glancing at Jeremy. "This might put a target on your back. They won't let you interfere easily."

Sophia shook her head. "They have money, weapons, influence. They threatened to harm my family if I tried to escape."

Jeremy crouched beside her, voice firm. "We'll keep you safe. No matter what."

A flicker of gratitude and fear shone in her eyes. "Why? You don't even know me."

He offered a reassuring smile. "Because helping people is the right thing. Doesn't matter if we've met before."

Lucas nodded from the console, his expression serious. "We can probably hook you up with some aid groups that help trafficking victims. They'll keep you off the radar until you can figure out legal status. Jeremy's done smaller rescues before, but this is bigger. A whole ring, maybe multiple diners or businesses. They might come for you too."

Jeremy straightened, adrenaline buzzing in his veins. "Let them come. If they're hurting people, someone has to stand against them."

Lucas rubbed his temples. "Just be careful, man. A purse snatcher is one thing. A criminal network is another."

Sophia's eyes brimmed with tears again. "I don't want anyone else getting hurt because of me."

Jeremy placed a gentle hand on her shoulder. "No one's blaming you. This is on them." He glanced at Lucas. "We can't let them keep doing this to others."

Lucas sighed, swiveling back to the screens. "All right. We dig deeper, see how widespread their operation is. We plan carefully—no reckless moves. And we protect Sophia until we find a permanent solution."

Silence wrapped around them for a moment. Outside, thunder rumbled faintly—or perhaps it was just the city's ceaseless activity. The diamond, perched on a side table, gave off a calm glow, its energy a quiet reminder of how Jeremy and Lucas had gained the power to "surf" the sky. In this lab, so many secrets converged.

Jeremy's gaze flicked between the diamond and Sophia, a swirl of emotions roiling. Only a short time ago, he'd scoffed at being some kind of hero, content to stay aloof while returning lost items or halting petty thieves. But tonight had showed a deeper darkness in the city. Traffickers using vulnerable people for profit. And it infuriated him.

Lucas cleared his throat, focusing on a newly displayed set of files. "Here's what I've got so far: multiple shell companies, restaurant fronts, fake paperwork. This network's big, Jer. If we poke the hornet's nest, we better be ready."

Jeremy exhaled slowly. "We will be. And if it means saving people like Sophia, I'm all in."

She peered up, anxiety etched into her young features. "Thank you," she whispered, voice trembling. "I can't believe this is real. You're risking yourselves for me."

Jeremy offered a small, reassuring nod. "For you, and for anyone else trapped in this mess."

Lucas gave a crooked grin. "Looks like we have ourselves an extended mission. Let's call it, I don't know, 'Waves of Justice' or something."

Jeremy barked a short laugh. "That's the best you can do?"

Lucas shrugged. "Hey, you're the surfer. I'm just the tech guy. But c'mon, it has a ring to it."

Sophia blinked through her tears, confusion momentarily replaced by a hesitant smile. "Waves of Justice?"

Jeremy shook his head in mock exasperation, but there was warmth in his eyes. "If it makes you happy, sure. Waves of Justice."

Lucas found a spare blanket and offered it to Sophia, guiding her to a small cot in the corner so she could rest. She settled in, likely exhausted from fear and adrenaline. Jeremy wandered toward a dim window, arms folded, staring at the city lights beyond. Flashes of lightning flickered on the horizon—a storm nearing, or perhaps just the reflection of more neon; he couldn't tell.

A swirl of thoughts crowded his mind. The discovery of a trafficking ring, the potential clash with dangerous criminals, and the possibility of harm to his family if these villains learned his identity. Yet, beneath all those fears, there was a resolute calm: *This is worth doing.* He pictured the relief in Sophia's eyes when she'd realized she could escape, and the rage in the diner owner's face when Jeremy stood up to him. If that man was just one cog in a larger machine, how many more victims were out there?

Footsteps approached behind him. Lucas spoke quietly so as not to wake Sophia. "So, tomorrow we start digging. We'll contact some local organizations—ones that help undocumented folks in trouble. We keep your sister out of this, keep your parents out of this. Maybe we find evidence, pass it to the authorities. Meanwhile, the diamond and the wave grid can give you an edge."

Jeremy faced him, expression set with determination. "I'm ready, Lucas. I didn't sign up for a big hero career, but if these people are exploiting kids and families, I can't turn my back."

Lucas reached out, giving Jeremy's shoulder a reassuring pat. "We do it carefully. If we're lucky, we free Sophia from their grasp and maybe shut down a chunk of this operation. Just … watch your back, okay?"

A faint smile tugged at Jeremy's lips. "Always."

They stood there for a while in companionable silence, the hum of electronics filling the lab. Sophia's soft breathing signaled she'd drifted into an uneasy sleep. The diamond glowed steadily, a testament to the power that had changed Jeremy's life. Outside, a fresh rumble of thunder rolled across the city, punctuating the night's tension.

Jeremy cast one final glance at the sleeping girl. Waves of Justice—the phrase hovered in his mind. Cheesy or not, it encapsulated their new mission: harnessing the wave grid's freedom to bring some measure of justice to those who had none. The city might never know the full story, but at least for Sophia, for others like her, they'd make a difference.

The night ebbed, leaving them on the brink of a larger fight than either had anticipated. The shadowy corners of Crescent Bay concealed a thousand untold stories, but this time, Jeremy and Lucas intended to shed light on at least one of them. Their vow hung unspoken in the air: to take on the traffickers, protect the vulnerable, and ride the waves of justice until no one could exploit those in need again.

Chapter 7

A week had passed since Jeremy saved Sophia from the hands of the Russian mobsters. The night air was thick with mist, drifting in from the coastline and settling over Crescent Bay like a gauzy veil. Neon lights reflected off the glistening streets, painting the fog in loose swirls of pastel color—soft blues, pinks, and yellows merging into each other. From high above, Jeremy watched these shifting patterns unfold as he cruised on his hidden wave grid, the hum of his hoverboard blending into the distant rumble of traffic.

He weaved silently between buildings, only the faintest glow betraying his presence. For a while, he let the city's pulsing energy guide him, relishing the freedom of coasting across the rooftops without a care—no immediate call for rescue, no petty criminals to intercept. It was just him, the swirl of mist, and the subdued neon glow.

A familiar crackle in his earpiece jolted him from his thoughts. "All quiet tonight?" Lucas asked, his voice filling Jeremy's helmet speakers with a mild buzz of static.

Jeremy smiled, leaning into a gentle turn that carried him across a darkened side street. "Almost too quiet," he murmured. "Feels like the city's holding its breath."

"Don't jinx it," came Lucas's wry reply. "The second you say something like that …" He trailed off, his tone shifting from casual to tense. "Uh-oh."

Jeremy's grin vanished. He angled the board slightly downward, skimming the lip of a roof. "What's that supposed to mean? I don't like 'uh-oh.'"

Lucas's fingers tapped audibly on a keyboard. "We've got movement. I see five black SUVs, tinted windows, with no license plates, heading your way fast, very fast—maybe two blocks behind you. I'm pulling up traffic cams now."

Frowning, Jeremy glanced over his shoulder, though he couldn't see much through the veil of fog. Then the haze parted just enough to reveal headlights, bright and slicing through the darkness like two blunt knives. The engine roared as the vehicle closed in, its growl echoing off the buildings.

"Yeah, I see them," Jeremy said under his breath, crouching on his board. His heart thudded harder. "Looks like we've got company."

"It looks like they spotted you," Lucas warned. "Go. Now."

The SUV screeched to a halt below him, tires screaming, and the doors were flung open. Three men tumbled out with practiced efficiency, each wielding a sleek black rifle that caught the streetlights in sporadic flashes. It took them all of three seconds to spot Jeremy suspended above the street—and to open fire.

Jeremy ducked in alarm as bullets pinged off the building's metal fire escape. "Okay, this just got a lot less fun."

He shifted his balance forward, sending the board hurtling down the block. Behind him came the staccato roar of automatic gunfire, peppering walls and shattering windows. The men shouted frantic orders, their footsteps pounding on the asphalt.

"One more SUV incoming." Lucas's voice cut through the din. "They're boxing you in from the other side."

"Terrific," Jeremy muttered, swinging the board into a tight left turn. Another black SUV roared around the corner ahead, headlights blazing. "They're definitely not the subtle type."

As the SUV slewed to a stop, more men spilled out. Jeremy recognized the same lethal composure—rifles up, scanning for their target. He felt a spike of anxiety. He had to outrun them, not engage in a direct fight on a foggy street.

"Time for Plan B," Lucas urged. "Go vertical. Construction site on your left. Five floors of scaffolding. That's your best shot."

Jeremy spotted it: a half-built tower of metal beams and concrete pillars looming in the haze. The building's frame jutted into the night sky like a half-finished cathedral. Gripping the board firmly, Jeremy angled himself toward the building.

Gunfire barked again, sparks flying off the sidewalk in bright bursts. "They're determined," Jeremy hissed, adrenaline spiking.

Hoisting the board's nose, he blasted forward, skimming dangerously close to the ground. He zipped past the mobsters, some of whom cursed in Russian as they scrambled to readjust their aim. Then he reached the scaffolding's base—a maze of steel and plywood rising into the gloom.

"Showtime," he muttered, crouching low. He pumped his legs, coaxing more speed from the board. With a clatter of metal, he rode up a supporting beam like a skater grinding a rail. Sparks danced where his board's edge met the steel, briefly illuminating the men below in harsh flashes.

"He's going up! Move, move, move!" one of the thugs shouted, voice echoing over the scaffolding's hollow interior.

Jeremy ascended in a series of smooth maneuvers: pivoting around pylons, hopping from one crossbeam to the next. Each section of scaffolding rang under his momentum. The men gave chase, rifles slung across their backs, but he had the advantage of the wave grid's intangible push, letting him glide upward faster than they could climb.

At last, he crested the top, launching himself in a graceful flip onto the adjacent building's rooftop. The board scraped as he landed, nearly pitching him forward. He wobbled, recovered, and then took off again. Below, the thugs stood on the highest scaffolding platform, powerless to stop him now. Jeremy vanished into the fog, a pale shape lost among the city's swirling lights.

***

The lab's interior felt tense when Jeremy returned. Lucas was glued to multiple monitors, scanning for any sign of the gang's vehicles. The diamond, resting on a special pedestal at the far end of the room, pulsed with its usual rhythmic glow—gentle but strangely reassuring.

Sophia sat curled on a faded couch, knees drawn to her chest. She wore an oversized sweatshirt that made her appear even smaller. Even from a distance, Jeremy could sense her distress. Her eyes were puffy from crying, and she stared into a chipped coffee mug as though it held the answers to her anxieties.

"How're we looking?" Jeremy asked, setting his hoverboard carefully against a wall. He tried to force a casual tone, but a tingle of nerves remained from the ambush.

Lucas didn't glance up. "Mob is definitely stepping up their game. Good thing you got out of there. Could've been a real mess."

Jeremy exhaled, running a hand through damp hair. "And Sophia?" he said softly, jerking his head in her direction.

Lucas shrugged, still watching his screens. "Not much progress. She's pretty shaken up. Hardly spoken a word all night."

Jeremy nodded. He crossed to the couch and crouched down in front of her, gentling his voice. "Hey. How're you holding up?"

At first, she didn't respond. Her gaze stayed locked on the mug, as though she was still lost in her own labyrinth of thoughts. Finally, she spoke, so quietly he almost missed it. "I'm ... trying."

He noticed the bruises on her arms, the shadows under her eyes. "You're safe here," he said gently. "We won't let them hurt you again."

She let out a faint, humorless laugh. "That's what they told me, too ... when I came to this country. 'You'll be safe,' they said. 'We'll help you find a better life.' And then they took my passport, locked me in a room, and made me work for nothing." Her voice cracked. "They said they owned me."

Jeremy felt a surge of anger on her behalf. "I'm sorry," he managed. "No one owns you. Not anymore."

Tears pooled in her eyes. She glanced at him, voice trembling. "They own everything. They don't just hurt people, they break them. You have no idea what they're capable of. They'll come for me. They'll come for you, too."

Jeremy's jaw tightened. "Then we'll fight them."

Sophia swallowed. "You can't fight them alone."

Across the room, Lucas cleared his throat. "She's right, you know. They're relentless."

Jeremy stared at the diamond's soft glow, a sense of resolve tightening his chest. "We'll figure something out," he said softly. "We have to."

***

Late into the night, after ensuring Sophia had calmed down a bit, Jeremy took one last patrol, riding the wave grid without any specific destination. The earlier gunfight replayed in his mind like a broken record. The mob's men had advanced rifles, bulletproof vehicles, and no hesitation to shoot. In the face of that kind of firepower, speed and skill only went so far. A single bullet at the wrong moment could end everything.

He found himself hovering over an intersection, neon signs casting a pinkish hue on the asphalt below. The city had quieted somewhat—bars shutting down, convenience stores closing. A low-level hum of traffic persisted, but the main hustle was done for the night.

Still, his mind raced. *We need a real plan. We can't just outrun them forever.* The wave grid gave him mobility, but it didn't solve the fundamental problem of dealing with violent criminals. Sure, he could dodge bullets, but how many shootouts could he survive before something went horribly wrong?

His stomach rumbled unexpectedly. He realized he'd missed dinner, too caught up in the chaos. A swirl of fried noodle smell drifted from a nearby corner, piquing his interest. He recognized a small Chinese restaurant—The Tiger and the Crane—advertised by a flickering neon sign. The place looked old-school, with peeling posters on the windows.

"Lucas," he said through the comms. "I'm grabbing a bite. Then I'll head back, okay?"

Lucas's voice crackled back. "You sure you want to risk it?"

Jeremy eyed the deserted alley behind the restaurant. "I'll be quick. Gotta eat."

With that, he dropped quietly into the alley, powering off the suit's more conspicuous features. He stashed his hoverboard on a flat rooftop overhead, out of sight, and stepped through a back entrance into The Tiger and the Crane.

The interior was small: maybe six booths, a row of stools at a counter, and a battered TV in the corner flickering with some late-night show. Red lanterns hung from the ceiling, casting a warm glow over faded kung fu movie posters plastered on the walls. The air smelled of ginger, soy, and sizzling garlic.

Behind the counter stood an elderly Chinese man with a lined face and keen, dark eyes. He wore a well-worn apron and wielded a wok over a roaring flame, flipping noodles with impressive speed. He barely glanced at Jeremy's entrance, barking in a thick accent, "Closing soon."

Jeremy slid onto a stool, ignoring the man's brusque tone. "I'll be fast," he said, breathing in the aroma. "Got any noodles left?"

The man snorted. "Always noodles. The best ones in town. What else do you think I sell?" With that, he scooped a ladleful of broth and dumped a fresh batch of noodles into the wok, stirring vigorously. After a minute, he plopped a steaming bowl in front of Jeremy. "Eat. Then go."

Jeremy picked up a spoon and chopsticks, diving in. The flavors burst on his tongue—savory, a bit spicy, and unbelievably comforting. He let out a satisfied groan. "You weren't kidding. Best noodles I've had in ages."

The cook only grunted in response, turning back to his station. The place was empty except for the two of them—closing time indeed.

Jeremy had devoured half the bowl when the front door chimed abruptly. He stiffened, glancing in the small restaurant mirror. Two men entered, broad-shouldered and reeking of trouble. They scanned the interior with a practiced gaze.

"We are closed," the cook snapped, not bothering to face them.

"Relax, old man," drawled the first intruder. He had a wiry frame and a thin-lipped grin that showed too many teeth. "We're just here to collect."

The second man smirked, flipping a chair aside. "Yeah, protection money. Gotta keep the streets safe, you know?"

Jeremy bristled, adrenaline snapping awake. *Mobsters? Or petty criminals? Probably the same ring that attacked me earlier.*

The cook spoke without turning around. "I told your boss I don't pay. I run my business alone."

A sneer curled across the thug's lips. "Bad decision, old man. Guess we'll have to teach you a lesson."

Jeremy tapped his chopsticks on the counter, drawing the men's attention. "Hey, guys, is that any way to talk to your host? Some of us are trying to eat here."

The second thug flicked his gaze to Jeremy. "None of your business, kid. Unless you want to lose those pretty teeth."

Rolling his eyes, Jeremy set down his bowl. "Seriously, you two bozos think you own this block? Newsflash: you don't."

Before the men could respond, the cook moved with startling speed. His hand lashed out, seizing the first thug's wrist. In a fluid motion, he twisted it sharply, forcing the man to cry out in surprise. Then the cook gave him a shove, sending him stumbling into the countertop.

"Hey—!" the second thug roared, lunging forward. But the cook sidestepped with uncanny agility, driving a swift kick into the back of the man's knee. The thug collapsed, and the cook shoved him to the ground with a dismissive push.

Jeremy stared, half risen from his stool, noodles forgotten. "What the ... that was—"

The old man tightened his apron with a scowl. "That was two fools getting exactly what they deserved."

One thug whimpered, cradling his wrist, while the other glowered from the tiled floor. With another bark from the cook—"Get out!"—they scrambled for the door, curses trailing behind them.

Jeremy blinked. "Dude, that was awesome."

The cook exhaled, turning back to the stove. "I don't like trouble in my shop."

Jeremy stood, eyes alight. "Where'd you learn that? Some kind of martial arts? You've gotta teach me."

The cook snorted. "I am cook, not teacher. Besides, you look like you are in a boy band, you are not kung fu material."

"Boy band?" Jeremy echoed, hands on his hips. "I am not in a boy band—in fact, I've got some moves myself, and I believe I've got what it takes … But man, the way you handled these guys. I did not expect that!"

"Exactly. You expect. I don't." The cook flipped his wok shut, wiping his hands. "Training you would be a waste of my time. I can see you got a big ego, boy band ego."

Jeremy huffed. "I'm serious. I need to be stronger, faster—I'm trying to help this city. People are in danger. You saw those punks. They work for someone bigger, and they keep terrorizing everyone."

He looked the cook in the eye and quietly said, "Please, Master. Teach me. I want to learn."

The cook eyed Jeremy up and down. Silence lingered. Finally, he gave a curt nod, almost grudgingly. "Fine. But no shortcuts. If you train here, you follow my rules. No whining, no skipping."

Jeremy's heart soared. "Yes! I promise!"

The cook tossed him a damp towel. "Clean up the mess here. First lesson: I break, you fix."

Jeremy laughed, but he dutifully grabbed the towel, thinking: *This is exactly what I need.*

***

After cleaning up the mess at The Tiger and the Crane, Jeremy headed back to the lab, where the atmosphere crackled with energy. Lucas's multiple holographic screens projected data streams, dispatch logs, and 3D diagrams. The diamond glowed softly, feeding into a series of newly installed conduits that trailed across the ceiling. Jeremy stepped inside, feeling a rush of excitement at the prospect of combining martial arts training with fresh tech.

"Welcome back," Lucas said, swiveling away from his main console. His eyes sparkled with pride. "We have a new toy for you."

Jeremy leaned against a bench, arms folded. "Oh?"

Lucas hit a command on his interface, and a sleek new suit slid out from behind a curtain, neatly mounted on a mannequin. Its lines were smooth and modern, exuding a hint of futuristic sheen. "Meet your updated outfit. I infused a layer of woven graphene that's bullet-resistant, at least against most small arms. Diamond energy helps reinforce it at the molecular level."

Approaching the mannequin, Jeremy ran a hand over the suit's surface. It felt light, pliable—nothing like the bulky Kevlar vests he'd seen cops wear. "This is insane," he said softly, tracing a seam that ran along the shoulder.

Lucas grinned. "Wait 'til you see the rest. The helmet interface now includes thermal imaging, so you can spot enemies hiding in the dark, plus a tactical overlay that marks threats and friendlies in real time. And the best part ..." He reached under the table, retrieving a slim metallic band no wider than a watch strap. "Behold: your new bracelet."

Jeremy raised an eyebrow. "What's it do?"

Lucas's grin widened. "Micro-missiles, for taking out, say, an approaching car or a pesky drone. A tiny laser cannon for heavier firepower—great for slicing through padlocks, maybe. And because I couldn't resist—"

"Let me guess," Jeremy cut in, laughing. "A retractable laser sword?"

Lucas shrugged, feigning nonchalance. "Guilty. I had the components lying around. Just be careful—it's less 'lightsaber' and more 'industrial cutting tool.' But it's plenty sharp."

Jeremy snapped the bracelet around his wrist, testing the fit. "I can't believe you did all this so fast."

Lucas turned back to his monitors, tapping in a few new settings. "We have to adapt. Those goons you ran into tonight? They'll be back, and they'll be worse. We can't rely on speed and luck alone."

Jeremy mulled over Sophia's warnings, the new threat from the mob, and his own near miss with gunfire. "I need every edge I can get. Especially if I'm about to be tangling with organized crime."

Lucas nodded, face grim. "Just promise me you'll be careful."

With a wry smile, Jeremy flexed his hand and felt the bracelet's mechanisms shift. "Careful is my middle name."

Lucas snorted. "Sure it is."

They exchanged a knowing look—part camaraderie, part dread for what lay ahead. Jeremy glanced again at the upgraded suit, the sparkling diamond lines running discreetly through its seams. The memory of bullets whizzing past him earlier was still fresh. Next time, he'd be better prepared.

Sometime later, after a quick test run of the new gear, Jeremy slipped out of the lab. Dawn was on the horizon, painting the edges of the sky a faint pink. Stifling a yawn, he realized he had to juggle normal life—school, chores, all that—while also training with a mysterious cook and waging a covert war against a dangerous mob.

Before he left, he glanced at Sophia, curled again on the couch, still fast asleep. A pang of empathy tugged at him. He'd do everything in his power to protect her—and any others like her who got caught in the mob's web.

Waving at Lucas, he set off into the pale morning. The board hummed as he ascended, the wave grid still faintly visible to him, guiding him homeward. The city below looked deceptively peaceful in the early light, but Jeremy knew trouble brewed under the surface.

The rising tide is coming, he thought. *And I'll be ready.*

At least now he had armor, new weapons, and soon—he hoped—a set of martial arts skills to match. The wind carried him gently toward the horizon, where the first rays of sunlight glinted off skyscraper windows. Another day dawned on Crescent Bay, and Jeremy Carter, newly determined, soared on ahead, preparing for the trials that would soon come crashing in like a relentless wave.

Chapter 8

The Tiger and the Crane was sealed for the night, its warm glow replaced by the hush of late-hour mystery. Only a single lantern flickered near the front window, casting elongated shadows across stacked chairs and vacant tables. During the day, the place bustled with life—cooks shouting orders, pots clanging, and customers chatting—but when the doors locked, it morphed into a private realm of instruction and trial.

Jeremy stood in the middle of the dining area, wearing an old T-shirt and sweatpants. His eyes wandered over the rearranged furnishings, which had been pushed against the walls to create an open floor space. He recalled how, just days before, he'd seen Mr. Zhang subdue two thugs here with minimal effort. Tonight, he was hoping to learn that secret for himself.

Mr. Zhang, the restaurant's owner, stood nearby. Barefoot and clad in a simple black tunic, he looked every bit the disciplined martial artist rather than a chef. His calm gaze carried a hint of challenge.

Jeremy shifted his weight, hands in his pockets. "So ... you're going to teach me how to fight like you did against those two guys?"

Mr. Zhang snorted softly. "Perhaps. But understand that kung fu is always tied to philosophy. It's not about throwing punches alone—any fool can do that. You must learn the deeper reason. Modern students ignore this, and it's stupid."

"Philosophy," Jeremy echoed, half curious, half skeptical. "Like … reading old texts instead of training?"

Mr. Zhang's expression hardened. "Yes. Because to be a great fighter, you must know yourself, know the world, and see how body and mind unite. He who knows others is wise; he who knows himself is enlightened. That's from the *Tao Te Ching*, verse thirty-three."

Jeremy raised an eyebrow. "So I need a philosophy lesson before I can punch stuff?"

"You need the Tao, not just a lecture," Mr. Zhang corrected. "It's not enough to be strong. If you lack humility and awareness, your power is hollow. Understand that, or you'll never truly fight."

Jeremy let out a small sigh but nodded. "All right. Let's hear it."

"First, you sit and breathe," Mr. Zhang instructed, pointing to a simple woven mat placed on the tiled floor.

Jeremy frowned. "Breathe? That's the big secret? I thought we'd start with some moves or—"

"Sit," Mr. Zhang repeated, voice brooking no argument. "Close your eyes. Inhale slowly through your nose, exhale through your mouth. If you can't control breath, you control nothing."

Jeremy dropped onto the mat, crossing his legs. He tried to breathe deeply, but his impatience gnawed at him after mere moments. "How long do I—"

Without warning, Mr. Zhang grabbed the collar of Jeremy's T-shirt and hoisted him upright. "You want a shortcut?" he snapped, dragging Jeremy through the restaurant's back door into a small courtyard. A koi pond shimmered under the moonlight.

"What?!" Jeremy yelped as Mr. Zhang shoved his head beneath the cold water. Shock pulsed through Jeremy's system. Instantly, he flailed, lungs crying out for air. Only after several seconds did Mr. Zhang yank him up again, allowing him to gulp fresh oxygen.

Jeremy coughed, water streaming down his face. "What the hell?" he shouted, wiping his eyes.

"When you cannot breathe, everything else is worthless," Mr. Zhang said coolly, stepping back. "Strength, speed—useless. Next time I say to focus on breath, do it. No arguments."

Jeremy glared, teeth chattering slightly. "Point taken," he rasped.

Mr. Zhang nodded, satisfied. "Good. Remember that feeling. He who stands on tiptoe cannot stand firm."

***

At dawn the following day, Jeremy returned—still annoyed about the dunking but oddly determined. The restaurant felt eerily calm in the predawn light, a single incense stick smoldering on a windowsill. Mr. Zhang stood with arms folded.

Jeremy chuckled. "I believe we covered a lot of breathing yesterday. Today, can we maybe get into some sparring? I'd like to see how all this works out. I told you I have my own moves, and with your breathing techniques I might be onto something here."

"You want to fight, yes?" Mr. Zhang said. "Very well. We'll fight. I'll use one finger … on my left hand."

Jeremy blinked. "Seriously? Just one finger?" He bristled at the implied insult.

Mr. Zhang lifted his left index finger, beckoning. "Attack me as you wish."

"Fine," Jeremy muttered, dropping into a guarded stance. He fired a quick punch. Mr. Zhang's finger brushed the strike aside with minimal effort. Another punch, another deflection. Jeremy tried a snap kick; the older man's finger tapped his shin mid-strike, sending it off course. Every move Jeremy made was neutralized by a seemingly impossible flick of a single finger.

Frustration built. Jeremy attempted a wide hook punch, hoping to catch Mr. Zhang off guard. The finger pressed the inside of Jeremy's elbow, twisting his punch into empty space. With a final fluid motion, Mr. Zhang poked Jeremy's supporting leg behind the knee. Jeremy toppled backward, hitting the floor with a thud.

"Ow!" he groaned. Mr. Zhang's finger hovered near Jeremy's temple, a mock finishing blow. "You've got to be kidding me."

"Pathetic," Mr. Zhang said, stepping back. "One finger is all it takes to beat you. Remember this humbling moment."

Humiliation burned Jeremy's cheeks. "But how?"

Mr. Zhang's expression remained impassive. "Because I'm not just using a finger—I'm using the Tao, my breath, your momentum, the angles around us. You rely on brute force. That's your downfall."

***

Over the next few days, Mr. Zhang put Jeremy through relentless drills. Early mornings began with stance training—horse stance, crane stance, single-leg balance. Jeremy's thighs ached, sweat pouring down his face as he tried to hold each position without collapsing. Whenever he faltered, Mr. Zhang rapped him lightly with a bamboo rod.

Later, they practiced striking: short Wing Chun punches, powerful Hung Gar sweeps, and quick mantis-style hooks. Jeremy's arms felt like lead by midday, but each repetition sharpened his form.

One afternoon, Mr. Zhang decided to showcase true mastery. He stacked a thick oak plank on two blocks and, with a single fluid strike, split the wood cleanly.

Jeremy stared, awed. "That's ... real oak," he breathed.

Mr. Zhang brushed sawdust from his hand. "Alignment, breath, and focus. Not mere muscle. 'Nothing in the world is as soft and yielding as water, yet for dissolving the hard and inflexible, nothing can surpass it.' I moved like water, finding the plank's weakest point."

Jeremy ran his hand over the split halves. "One day I'll be able to do that, right?"

Mr. Zhang nodded. "When you stop forcing yourself and start flowing."

Evenings often ended with meditation. Mr. Zhang would sit cross-legged in the silent dining area, eyes shut, shoulders relaxed. A subtle hum sometimes filled the air, and Jeremy sensed a faint static tension that raised the hair on his arms.

One night, curiosity got the better of him, and he reached out to tap Mr. Zhang's shoulder. A small spark crackled, causing Jeremy to jerk back with a startled yelp.

Mr. Zhang opened one eye. "You felt my qi. Disturb a meditating man's energy, and you might get a jolt."

Jeremy massaged his tingling fingers. "So … you become electric?"

Mr. Zhang smirked. "In a sense. My mind, breath, and spirit align. The energy resonates. You must approach gently, or you break the harmony."

"And that's part of kung fu, too?" Jeremy asked, still stunned.

"Kung fu, Tao, breath—it's all connected," Mr. Zhang replied. "He who knows others is wise; he who knows himself is enlightened. Once you harness your internal energy, it can manifest physically."

Between endless stance drills and repeated attempts at the single-finger fight, Mr. Zhang hammered home the philosophy behind every movement. He made Jeremy recite lines from the *Tao Te Ching* each morning. Jeremy found himself drawn to these ancient verses, though some remained cryptic.

"'When two great forces oppose each other, the victory will go to the one that knows how to yield,'" Mr. Zhang would quote. "In fighting, if you meet force with force, you risk breaking. Yield like water, let the opponent's energy pass, and then strike."

Jeremy tried to apply this in sparring. He'd attempt to sense Mr. Zhang's incoming moves, deflecting rather than resisting. Though he still ended up on his backside often, he sensed incremental improvement.

Occasionally, Mr. Zhang delivered unexpected lessons—like making Jeremy stand blindfolded in the courtyard listening for footsteps, or forcing him to do fingertip push-ups until his arms shook. "Pain is good," Mr. Zhang would say blandly. "It means you have room to grow."

One humid afternoon, Mr. Zhang decided to test Jeremy's progress again with the single-finger duel. Jeremy squared up, recalling the humiliations of past attempts. But now he'd internalized some of the Tao: to flow like water, to yield rather than clash.

He opened with a measured Wing Chun punch. Mr. Zhang's finger batted it aside. Jeremy slid into a Hung Gar stance, unleashing a powerful mid-level strike. The finger pressed the back of Jeremy's elbow, diverting the blow. Gritting his teeth, Jeremy shifted quickly into a mantis hook aimed at Mr. Zhang's ribs, hoping to exploit a new angle. For an instant, it almost connected—until Mr. Zhang nudged Jeremy's thigh with his finger, knocking the younger man off-balance.

Jeremy gasped, forced to break off. He stumbled, but didn't fall this time. A flicker of triumph: *He didn't put me on the ground immediately.* Encouraged, he pivoted and tried a low kick. Again, the finger found a nerve point behind his knee, sending him collapsing to the tiles.

Panting, Jeremy stayed down, waiting for the finishing blow.

Mr. Zhang's finger hovered an inch from Jeremy's temple. Then he lowered it. "Better," he conceded, with a slight grin. "You made me move. That's improvement."

Despite the bruises, Jeremy's heart soared. "I'll keep trying."

Mr. Zhang nodded. "Yes. Keep trying."

At day's end, Mr. Zhang handed Jeremy a small, worn copy of the *Tao Te Ching*, its cover frayed at the edges. "Memorize a verse a day," he said. "Reflect on how it applies to kung fu—and to life."

Jeremy flipped through pages filled with poetic lines about water, emptiness, yielding, and nature. One verse in particular caught his eye: "He who knows others is wise; he who knows himself is enlightened." He recognized it as the concept Mr. Zhang repeated.

"So ... that's basically the core? Know myself, know the world, fight better?"

Mr. Zhang chuckled softly. "Yes, but deeper than that. The Tao is about harmony—the unity of mind and body—the very thing you need if you ever hope to beat me with more than just a finger."

Jeremy cracked a grin. "One day, I'll do it with *no* fingers."

Mr. Zhang smirked. "We shall see."

Late that evening, after an exhausting session of bridging exercises and stance work, Mr. Zhang led Jeremy into a back storeroom. He picked out a thick oak beam, far denser than the planks Jeremy had practiced on before.

Setting it between two crates, Mr. Zhang inhaled smoothly, then exhaled, letting his shoulders loosen. Jeremy felt a hush, as though the air anticipated something. With a swift, precise strike of his palm, Mr. Zhang split the beam in two. The impact echoed in the confined space.

Jeremy stepped forward, gaping at the clean break. "How ...? That's insane."

Mr. Zhang shook off dust from his hand. "Alignment, breath, flow. Nothing in the world is as soft and yielding as water, yet for dissolving the hard and inflexible, nothing can surpass it. I move like water. The wood stands rigid. Who wins?"

Awe rippled through Jeremy. "I'll get there someday."

"You might—if you keep the Tao in your heart."

Not long after, Jeremy encountered Mr. Zhang meditating in near-total darkness. The air thrummed with an undercurrent of energy. This time, Jeremy approached more cautiously. He placed his hand near Mr. Zhang's shoulder, pausing inches away to sense the subtle static. It felt like a gentle buzz on his fingertips.

Mr. Zhang opened his eyes, letting the energy dissipate. "You're calmer now. Less disruptive. That's good."

Jeremy nodded. "It's incredible what you can do just by sitting there."

Mr. Zhang gave a faint smile. "It's called internal harmony. Even in meditation, if you push too hard, you break the flow. Approach gently, you join it."

***

Finally, one night—after what felt like endless stance drills, single-finger humiliations, and oak plank demonstrations—Mr. Zhang and Jeremy settled at a small table near the kitchen, each sipping tea. The only light came from a battered lamp overhead, casting long shadows on the walls.

Jeremy still couldn't believe that a few weeks ago, he'd literally battled the Russian mob to save Sophia—and nearly got himself pulverized in the process. Now, things were quieter, but the quiet felt charged, like the calm before a storm. The crew had been keeping a low profile, laying out their next move in this ever-growing mission.

In the mornings, Jeremy had his routine down to an art form: he'd wake up before sunrise, slip out of the house, and train until it was time for school. After the first bell rang, he'd usually meet up with Lucas in the hall. Sometimes he'd skip a class to catch some waves at the beach.

By afternoon, they'd regroup in the lab, where Sophia was knee-deep in her research. She refused to let the Russian mob get away with their crimes, especially after what they'd done to her. With Lucas's help—and the unbelievable hacking power of that mysterious diamond—she was gathering piles of intel on Sergei Ubarov. According to what she'd pieced together, Sergei was no ordinary thug. He used to be a double agent for the CIA, helping them track Bin Laden in Afghanistan. Somewhere along the line, the agency had conveniently turned a blind eye to his human and drug trafficking.

That knowledge made everyone uneasy; this was way bigger than stolen wallets. Sergei was a serious threat, and messing with him was like lighting a match in a room full of gasoline. They all knew there was no turning back. This was their fight now.

While Sophia dug into more files and leads, Lucas spent every spare minute tinkering with the grid and suit he'd developed. It was already impressive, but Lucas was obsessed with making it even stronger, even deadlier, if push came to shove.

Jeremy blew on his cup, sore muscles protesting each movement. He thought of Sophia rescued from traffickers and the criminal threats prowling Crescent Bay's streets. The more he understood kung fu and the Tao, the more he sensed that simply punching harder wouldn't be enough against heavily armed or ruthless enemies.

Mr. Zhang set down his cup. "Your talk about 'taming the tiger'? That's an internal battle. The tiger is your anger, your impatience, your fear. Conquer that, and external foes are easier."

Jeremy nodded slowly. "I'm starting to see that. Sometimes my own frustration is worse than any punch you land."

Mr. Zhang chuckled. "Then keep training. One day, you may stand firm against the enemy, not because you're strong, but because you *flow*. Water is unstoppable."

Jeremy recalled the verse about water dissolving hardness. "Yeah. I'll be like water, right?"

Mr. Zhang inclined his head. "Exactly." He paused, sipping tea. "Your journey is far from over. But tonight, you've taken a step forward. Rest now. Return tomorrow."

Jeremy left The Tiger and the Crane with the *Tao Te Ching* under one arm, stepping onto deserted streets washed by the faint glow of distant lamps. Overhead, the sky hinted at dawn—a pale line along the horizon. He thought about the koi pond dunk, the single-finger fights, the broken oak beam, and that electrifying meditation. All of it wove a tapestry of lessons about humility, breath, and the synergy of mind and body.

He found the rooftop where he'd stashed his hoverboard. Sliding onto it, he activated the wave grid.

The city lights spread beneath him like a sparkling map, each block a testament to the challenges yet to come. Whether facing petty thieves or dangerous criminals, Jeremy now grasped that strength alone wasn't victory. He needed the Tao's guidance—the unity of thought, breath, and action that Mr. Zhang embodied.

A wry grin tugged at his mouth. "Time to be water," he murmured. With a gentle push, he soared into the predawn sky, body still aching from training but spirit quietly buoyed by new clarity.

Down below, The Tiger and the Crane's lanterns flickered in the breeze, sentinel-like, awaiting the next night's secret lessons. Jeremy knew he had a long road of discipline and introspection ahead. But for once, he felt ready—ready to tame the tiger within, to flow around obstacles, and to rise above the fear that once chained him.

As he vanished into the early-morning hush, the words of Mr. Zhang echoed in his mind: "Kung Fu is philosophy in motion. Understand the Tao, and no enemy—within or without—can truly conquer you."

Chapter 9

Stars glimmered faintly through the smoggy glow of Crescent Bay as Jeremy sat cross-legged in Mr. Zhang's backyard garden. Early-morning air clung to the city, and the hush of predawn lent a surreal calm to the small walled courtyard. A faint breeze stirred the bamboo stalks, and ancient stone lanterns circled the koi pond, reflecting soft moonlight across the water's surface.

Jeremy inhaled deeply, trying to anchor his mind in the present. The aches in his thighs and calves lingered from yesterday's stance drills, where Mr. Zhang had pushed him well past his usual limits. Each time he felt the protest of his muscles, he recalled Mr. Zhang's reminder to *breathe*, letting oxygen reach every tense fiber.

"Breathe deeper." Mr. Zhang's voice cut through the stillness, calm but unyielding. "There is tension in your back and shoulders."

Jeremy tried to exhale the tightness away. "It's not easy to 'breathe deeper' when my legs feel like they're on fire from all those stances."

"That's why you must practice," Mr. Zhang said, his tone edged with gentle command. "A warrior fights not only with his arms and legs, but with his breath and his mind. The body alone cannot prevail."

A short laugh escaped Jeremy. He opened his eyes, scanning the serene garden. "Yeah, but how is any of this supposed to help me deal with all the gangsters terrorizing our city?"

Mr. Zhang's quiet chuckle made the lanterns' reflections shimmer. "Because you still fixate on outward strength. Real strength begins inside." He reached out, tapping Jeremy's chest lightly. "When the tiger comes, your breath will keep you steady."

Jeremy let out a long sigh but forced himself to remain seated, letting the silence envelop him. The soft trickle of water in the pond almost lulled him into a state of relaxation—until his phone buzzed.

He opened his eyes with a frown. "Who on earth calls at five-thirty in the morning?"

"Maybe your girlfriend," Mr. Zhang teased, a rare grin flickering across his face.

Jeremy smirked, but the expression vanished at once as he saw the caller ID: Lucas. A jolt of alarm coursed through him—Lucas never called this early unless something dire had happened.

He snatched up the phone. "Lucas? What's going on?"

"Jeremy!" Lucas's normally steady voice trembled with fear. "They found us! The lab—they broke in!"

Jeremy leaped to his feet, nearly stumbling over the small mat he'd been sitting on. "What? Who? The mob?"

"Yes!" Lucas's words tumbled out, panicked. "They tore the place apart. They *took* Sophia, and they have the diamond!"

A chill stabbed through Jeremy's gut. "Are you hurt?"

"Don't worry about me!" Lucas snapped. "They're getting away. We need you. *Now!*"

Jeremy turned to Mr. Zhang, eyes wide with alarm. "My friend is in huge trouble, Master. I have to go."

Mr. Zhang observed him a moment, expression unreadable. Then he nodded. "Go. Keep your focus. Let the Tao guide you."

Jeremy didn't wait for further advice. He grabbed his old skateboard, the only board he had at Mr. Zhang's place, and tore out through the garden's gate.

***

The lab, or what was left of it, made Jeremy's stomach churn. The doorframe had been blasted apart, jagged wooden shards strewn across the entry. Inside, dangling wires sparked, and multiple screens hung crooked, their glass shattered. The acrid stench of burnt plastic lingered. The place looked as though a hurricane had torn through.

Lucas slumped against a wall, clutching his ribs, a cut on his forehead bleeding sluggishly. His phone lay shattered nearby. He winced, glasses askew, but waved Jeremy off. "I'm okay. They blindsided me." His breath hitched. "They knew *exactly* what they wanted."

Jeremy's eyes raked over the destruction. "How did they find this place?"

Lucas shook his head, voice thick with anger. "No idea. It wasn't random. They took the diamond, shut the grid down. And … they grabbed Sophia."

A spark of horror flared in Jeremy's chest. "But how—?"

"They must have had inside info," Lucas said through clenched teeth. "This wasn't guesswork."

Jeremy's throat tightened. He recalled how vital the diamond was to powering his wave grid. "So … no diamond, no grid. My best advantage is gone."

Lucas grimaced, pushing himself upright with a groan. "We can't focus on that. We have to find Sophia. Check her phone's location. If they haven't destroyed it, we might be able to track them."

Jeremy gave a curt nod, pacing nervously as Lucas limped toward his battered console. Sparks flickered when he tried to power it, but one cracked screen flickered on. He typed quickly, sweat shining on his brow.

Finally, a digital map appeared, albeit with glitchy lines. A small red dot blinked, moving north at a steady speed. "She's on the highway, heading out of the city," Lucas said, voice taut with urgency.

Jeremy's gaze darted to his high-tech surfboard leaning in a corner, half covered by fallen debris. Useless now. He grabbed it out of habit, then dropped it with a frustrated growl. "No waves, no ride." He turned, spotting his battered skateboard propped against the far wall. It had been months since he'd relied on that old board, but it was better than nothing. He snatched it up, testing the wheels. "This'll have to do."

Lucas slumped back, pressing a hand to his ribs. "Hurry, they're already twenty minutes ahead. I'll do what I can from here."

Jeremy nodded, eyes burning with resolve. "Hang in there."

With that, he sprinted out the ruined door, adrenaline fueling each step.

***

He sped down deserted side streets on the skateboard, mind racing. The sky was a dull gray, the sun barely peeking over the skyline. Streetlamps still glowed in patchy intervals, and the city felt eerily calm. Jeremy's phone tracked Sophia's location in real time, the blinking dot receding north.

They're taking her outside city limits.

Reaching a main road, he spotted a few vehicles heading onto the freeway. He kicked off the asphalt, weaving between them, determined to find a fast ride. An older SUV roared past, merging onto the highway ramp. Perfect. He gritted his teeth, pushing hard, and latched onto the SUV's rear bumper. The sudden jolt almost tore the board from under him.

"Jeremy," came Lucas's voice through the phone's speaker, "this is risky—even for you."

Jeremy hung on, bending his knees to absorb shocks. "Don't care—I'm a bit out of options."

The SUV accelerated onto the freeway, speed climbing. Jeremy's legs shook from the strain, but he forced calm. He remembered Mr. Zhang's words about breath under duress, letting tension flow out with each exhalation. Cars whooshed past, horns blaring in alarm at the sight of a skateboarder clinging to a bumper.

Up ahead, a city bus trundled along in the same direction. Jeremy released the SUV, coasting on momentum, then grabbed the bus's side mirror as it roared by. He glimpsed astonished faces pressed to the windows. *Let them stare.* He had no time to be polite— Sophia's life hung in the balance.

After several miles, the bus slowed at a rural gas station near the city's northern edge. Jeremy hopped off, the skateboard rattling to a stop. Checking his phone, he saw Sophia's dot far ahead, crossing from suburban roads into a mountainous stretch. The only route leading there was a steep, twisting highway cutting through pine forests.

Even clinging to cars, he might not catch them in time.

Need a faster method.

Then he spotted it: a neglected dirt bike leaning by the gas station's side, half hidden by a tangle of weeds. The keys hung from the ignition, covered in dust.

"Lucas," Jeremy hissed into his phone. "There's a dirt bike here, left with keys. I'm … borrowing it."

Lucas, still sounding pained, sighed. "If you have to. But be careful."

Jeremy mounted the bike, twisting the key. The engine sputtered, coughing black smoke before roaring awake. "I'll bring it back," he muttered, not entirely sure if that was true. With a rev, he tore out of the station, gravel spitting behind him.

The road soon climbed into forested hills. Towering pines flanked the highway, their branches forming a dense canopy that filtered the weak morning light. Jeremy pushed the dirt bike as fast as he dared, phone strapped to his arm so he could watch Sophia's dot creep deeper into mountainous terrain. The crisp air bit at his cheeks, a stark contrast to the city's muggy gloom.

"Lucas, they're heading up some old mountain road. Possibly a private property or lodge?"

Lucas's voice crackled. "I'm pulling any local maps I can. Looks like there's a few old cabins up there—some rumored to be used by criminals. Just watch yourself."

The road narrowed to a steep dirt trail, ruts threatening to topple the bike if he wasn't careful. Jeremy forced steady breaths, remembering Mr. Zhang's emphasis on calm even amid chaos. Anxiety chewed at him: Sophia could be in grave danger, the diamond lost, the mob well-armed. Yet he clung to discipline, refusing to let fear hijack his focus.

Eventually, Jeremy spotted the glow of headlights through the trees. He slowed, pulling off behind a dense grove of pines. From his hidden vantage point, he saw a row of black SUVs winding up a narrow dirt drive. The path led to a large, fortress-like structure perched on the mountainside—log walls, tall windows glowing faintly in the dawn.

He killed the engine, heart thudding in his ears. Men with rifles stood around the SUVs, scanning the perimeter. Jeremy's eyes darted around until he spotted Sophia being dragged from one vehicle, her hands bound, face etched in terror. Rage and dread coalesced in his chest.

He pressed a finger to his earpiece. "Lucas," Jeremy whispered, voice taut with urgency. "I found them."

Chapter 10

The mountain wind cut through the trees, carrying a bone-deep chill and the faint scent of fuel and damp stone. Jeremy crouched behind a jagged boulder, his breath forming small clouds in the frosty air. Up ahead, a looming fortress of steel and concrete reared out of the darkness, its walls coiled in barbed wire and floodlights sweeping the perimeter. Armed guards moved like shadows along the ramparts, rifles clutched tight.

The headset in Jeremy's ear had gone silent over half an hour ago. No Lucas giving him real-time updates. No last-minute jokes or tips. Just Jeremy, alone in the cold, facing an impossible mission. *No wave grid*, he thought grimly. No advanced board powered by the diamond. That same diamond—and Sophia—were somewhere in that fortress, taken by the Russian mob after their brutal raid on Lucas's lab.

He pulled the collar of his stolen guard's jacket higher around his neck. It was baggy enough to give a passing illusion of legitimacy in low light, but snug in all the wrong places. Every rational thought told him this was madness. He had no plan, no backup, no technology to bail him out. But he had to go. Sophia needed him.

***

The floodlights swept across the pine trees in slow arcs, carving the forest into patches of stark illumination and deeper blackness. Jeremy timed their cycles, then darted between boulders and tree trunks, each footstep muffled by the damp needles underfoot. His heart thundered at each near miss—one slip, and the guards would see him. But he pressed on, eventually reaching a vantage point behind a large crate near a side entrance.

A delivery truck sat nearby, workers unloading crates while two guards smoked and chatted. Overhead, a harsh lamp revealed a keypad by the steel door. Jeremy rolled his eyes inwardly. *Of course it's locked.* His gaze snagged on a clipboard attached to the truck's side. He crept over and flipped through pages until a scribbled code popped out.

Classic incompetent villains, he mused, lips twitching in a humorless grin.

He crept back to the door, punched in the numbers, and exhaled relief when the lock hissed open. Sliding inside, he let it seal behind him. A faint hum of machinery pervaded the narrow corridor, the air colder than outside. A swirl of tension gripped his gut.

This is only step one.

The fortress's interior resembled a claustrophobic warren of steel corridors, each turn identical—bare walls, exposed ducts, flickering fluorescent lamps. Jeremy moved with agonizing caution, pressing against walls when distant footsteps echoed. At one point, he glimpsed a guard passing an intersection. Heart pounding, he forced himself to breathe quietly until the man vanished.

Jeremy clenched his fists, guilt churning in his gut. *I've got to get Sophia out of here,* he told himself. *This is on me. Lucas and I weren't careful enough, and now she's paying the price.* He took a shaky breath. *I have to fix this ... and I have to do it now.*

After a few turns, he spotted three more guards at a corridor's far end. He tried to slip back, but one guard spotted him. "Hey! You—stop!"

No time to bluff. Jeremy bolted. Shouts followed, boots pounding in pursuit. A frantic voice rang out: "Sound the alarm!" A moment later, a klaxon whooped, red lights strobing down the halls.

Jeremy's adrenaline spiked. *They know I'm here.* He tore down the corridor, breath coming in ragged bursts.

He careened around a bend, searching desperately for a side door.

Another squad of guards burst through it before he could reach it, rifles leveled at him. Skidding to a stop, he tried to raise his hands, but a rifle butt slammed into his stomach, stealing the air from his lungs. Another blow cracked against his head. The world spun, blackness swallowing him up.

***

When he regained consciousness, pain flooded his body. Each breath felt raw, and the back of his skull pulsed with a vicious ache. He lay on damp stone, the smell of mildew clogging his nose. A soft drip echoed in the darkness. With effort, he pushed himself upright.

"Jeremy?" came Sophia's voice, trembling. She was huddled against the wall of the cramped cell, her eyes wide and fearful. Dust smeared her cheeks, and her wrists bore fresh zip ties.

Jeremy's heart soared the moment he spotted Sophia—safe and sound. Seeing her alive, he felt like he could finally breathe again.

"Sophia?" he croaked, crawling toward her. "You okay?"

"I'm … I'm fine," she managed, though tears brimmed in her eyes. "They took the diamond. And I haven't seen Lucas since the raid. I—"

Another voice interrupted. "I'm here," it said tersely.

Jeremy whipped around to see Lucas, arms folded, in a corner, his glasses askew. He looked exhausted, clothes dirty but no glaring injuries.

"Lucas? You got caught, too?" Jeremy blinked. "How'd you even—?"

"I took an Uber," Lucas said flatly, not meeting Jeremy's gaze.

"Seriously?" Jeremy asked him. "You actually Ubered here?"

"Yes," Lucas said. "I am in a wheelchair, you know. I can't just skate here."

"No, no, I totally get it," Jeremy said. "I just never thought stopping crime could be so convenient. Did you also stop for snacks?"

Lucas and Sophia looked at each other, amused; that was typical of Jeremy, being a smart-ass on any occasion. But they all knew there was no time for comedy now. Their situation was dire.

Before Jeremy could ask more, heavy footsteps resounded in the hall. The cell door swung open with a clang, revealing Sergei—a hulking figure whose scarred face dripped arrogance. Another man shuffled behind him, hair streaked with gray, guilt etched into every line of his face. Jeremy's stomach sank at the broken expression on Lucas's face.

"Dad?" Lucas whispered, voice cracking. His father avoided Lucas's gaze, shoulders slumped in shame. "You … you told them about the lab?"

Sergei smirked, gesturing theatrically. "He wanted to 'protect his boy.' So I made him a little promise—hand over the diamond, and you'd be left unharmed."

Lucas's father rubbed his eyes wearily. "I—I thought it would end the danger. I didn't know they'd—"

"So you knew what we were doing all this time?" Lucas cried. "You were spying on us?"

"Yes, I knew what you were doing, and as long as it was a harmless teen game, I didn't mind, but after seeing you guys messing up with the mob, I decided to call it quits. I knew it would end badly," his father said.

"Why didn't you just talk to me?" Lucas shouted, hurt fueling his anger. "You gave them the diamond. Now they can do anything with that power!"

Sergei's eyes glinted with dark amusement. "Yes, indeed. Let's show you what your diamond has built." At his nod, guards heaved open a steel door at the far side of the room. The ground quaked as something massive stepped into view.

A towering armored suit lumbered forward, thick steel plates welded together into a monstrous exoskeleton. Sparks danced across riveted seams. The diamond rested at its core, sealed in a cylinder that glowed with eerie, pulsing light, cables snaking outward to the suit's bulky limbs. Jeremy noted the array of weaponry: twin missile launchers perched on the shoulders, a rotating minigun on one arm, and a serrated claw on the other. Tracks reminiscent of a tank anchored its legs.

"Isn't this suit a beauty? All I needed was something incredible to finish it," Sergei said, voice dripping with pride. "The ultimate weapon."

Lucas's father staggered forward, face pale. "You said—" he began, but Sergei's claw knocked him aside with a brutal swipe. He cried out, crashing to the floor.

Lucas lunged for the bars with a cry of "Dad!" But the cell's iron rods held him in place. "Hiding behind a metal monster?" he snapped at Sergei. "You're a coward."

Sergei chuckled over the suit's external speakers. "Coward? Hardly. This is real power, genius boy."

In the corner of the cell, Jeremy closed his eyes, ignoring the burning throb of bruises across his body. He tried to tune out Sergei's bragging, focusing on the diamond's chaotic presence. He could feel its raw energy from across the room—wild, uncontained, and now fueling that monstrous suit. The recollection of Mr. Zhang's teaching welled up. *You can harness power if you keep your mind calm.*

He began slowing his breath, inhaling deeply despite the agony each movement caused. Lucas hissed, "Jeremy, now is not the time to meditate!" but Jeremy pressed on, blocking out everything but the diamond's pulse. Each exhalation chipped away at the fear constricting his chest, letting him reach for the swirling chaos of energy from a distance.

An overwhelming surge of force blazed through his mind. He gasped, muscles jolting as if he'd been electrocuted. The diamond's violent hum roared in his senses, beckoning him, testing him. *Don't fight it— channel it.* He pictured the calm pond in Mr. Zhang's garden, the ripples of water settling when the wind died.

Sophia's voice rang out, frantic. "Jeremy! Please— stop!"

But he continued. Warmth flared in his core, swiftly turning into scorching heat that made every nerve scream. His breathing slowed, eyes shut tight, sweat beading on his forehead. Then, abruptly, a golden glow shimmered around him, faint at first, then growing brighter. Lucas and Sophia stared as the cell bars began to vibrate.

With a soft hiss, the metal softened under invisible pressure. Molten droplets slid down the bars, dripping onto the floor in glowing pools. The iron parted, leaving a gap wide enough for Jeremy to step through.

He turned to them, eyes glowing with an inner light. "Stay behind me," he said calmly.

***

Sergei's guards reacted first, opening fire with rifles. Time seemed to distort for Jeremy; the diamond's power sharpened his perception. Bullets cut through the air like slow trails of light. He sidestepped, the golden aura around him sparking as stray rounds disintegrated upon contact.

A wave of his hand sent an arc of energy lashing out, knocking the guards off their feet. They crashed into steel crates, rifles clattering. One guard tried to scramble up, but Jeremy moved in a blur, disabling him with a single glowing strike to the jaw.

Sergei howled, powering up the suit. Engines whined, the minigun on one arm spinning up with a guttural roar. "Try dodging this," he snarled.

A hail of bullets erupted, tearing at the floor and walls. Jeremy darted aside, each bullet streaking by in slow motion. He touched the nearest one with a glimmering fingertip, and it disintegrated into a puff of sparks. He moved with uncanny grace, each step guided by the diamond's blazing energy. The bullets never touched him—time was too sluggish for the muzzle's fury to lock onto his position.

He vaulted onto a column of crates, glaring up at Sergei's monstrous suit. The machine seemed unstoppable—until Jeremy felt its flawed design. The diamond's raw power was too much for the suit's crude engineering. Sparks leaped along cables, and mechanical joints groaned under the strain.

Sergei launched a missile, but the entire launcher sputtered, jammed by an overload of the diamond's energy. Instead of firing, it sent a shower of sparks bursting from the shoulder mount. Sergei roared, swinging the claw in frustration, smashing debris. He tried pivoting the minigun, but the feed jammed. Another wave of bullets spattered the ceiling in a chaotic arc.

"No ... why won't it stabilize?!" Sergei bellowed over the suit's speakers. The machine lurched, half frozen by its own meltdown. Cables popped and fizzled along its torso, arcs of electricity dancing between them.

Jeremy seized that moment, leaps bridging the gap in slow-motion elegance. Each footstep glowed. He soared onto the suit's arm, ignoring the searing heat.

Sergei struggled to aim the claw, but time was too slow from Jeremy's perspective—he sidestepped it with ease, each dodge an effortless flow.

The diamond's presence hammered in Jeremy's mind. *I can't just tear it out without touching it*, he thought. But the meltdown in the suit was unstoppable. If he simply channeled the energy from afar, he might short the entire rig. In a single breath, he closed his eyes, letting out a silent invocation of calm. *Inside reflects the outside*, he recalled.

He inhaled. His aura brightened, golden flares dancing around him. From a distance of a few feet, he focused on the diamond's frantic pulse inside the suit's chest. The swirling power responded to his calm mind. He felt the diamond's energy shift toward him, straining the cables that tried to contain it. The suit convulsed, each joint sparking in protest.

"No," Sergei gasped as the machine's lights flickered. The diamond's violent radiance streamed away from the rig, unraveling the weapon systems. One launcher cracked, half dropping off in a burst of flame. The claw jerked uncontrollably, smashing a row of monitors.

Jeremy felt the diamond's essence surge, bridging his consciousness with its molten core. Time ground to a near standstill. Guards retreated in slow steps, bullets drifting as silver lines in the gloom. Sergei's face behind the cockpit's tinted glass twisted in an agonized roar, though no sound emerged yet.

In the hush, Jeremy breathed, letting the energy swirl around him, not fighting the pain but letting it pass through him.

He raised a trembling hand. From a distance, he guided the diamond's chaotic energy to detach from the harness. The cables frayed, each fiber snapping under invisible tension. Sparks cascaded, each droplet of molten metal arcing in slow motion. The suit's plating peeled away like foil, collapsing inwards.

Sergei, freed from the cockpit's protective cage, stumbled out, eyes wide with terror. He fled through a side door, leaving the shattered husk of the machine behind. The meltdown reached its climax, sending a final wave of sparks and a dull thud as the exoskeleton caved in on itself. Smoke and static discharge blanketed the corridor.

Some guards found their nerve, firing at Jeremy again. But he still moved in the diamond's slowed time. Bullets hovered, muzzle flashes lingering like flickering strobe lights. He stepped through them, each motion elegant, a dancer in a hail of death. He felt the diamond's scorching heat behind his eyes, each blink a struggle. Yet he pressed on, disarming guards with glowing strikes that left them unconscious and battered on the floor.

Sergei was already aware of his defeat and knew he was next; he quickly opened a hidden trapdoor in the floor and climbed down, but not before exclaiming, "This isn't over, surfer boy!" as he fled.

Sophia and Lucas took cover behind toppled crates, shielding Lucas's father, who lay dazed. Blood spattered the walls from stray shots. The corridor reeked of gunpowder, adrenaline, and fear. Every sense screamed at Jeremy to stop, yet he persisted, harnessing the diamond's unyielding power.

At last, the final guard collapsed under a swift blow, rifle tumbling from limp fingers. The corridor was awash in moans of wounded men, flickering alarm lights, and swirling smoke from the meltdown.

Jeremy staggered, aura flickering. The time-slow effect faltered, normal speed reasserting itself. He nearly collapsed, a raw cry escaping his throat.

Sophia rushed out, tears glistening. "Jeremy!" she cried, arms hooking around his waist as he swayed. Lucas scrambled forward, supporting him from the other side. The diamond's glow still clung to Jeremy like a shimmering halo, but it was fading fast, each pulse weaker.

Jeremy couldn't speak, every muscle trembling in exhaustion. *Inside … calm … outside.*

He summoned one last breath, ignoring the searing pain in his lungs. Gently, he eased the diamond's chaotic energy away from his body, letting it settle into a dim hum. Each second felt like an eternity as he forcibly quelled the unstoppable storm inside him.

When it was done, the diamond hung in midair for a heartbeat, then dropped lightly to the floor, an inert glow left in its center. Jeremy's legs gave out. He collapsed into Sophia's arms, his breathing ragged.

"Inside reflects the outside," he murmured, lips curving in a faint, exhausted smile. Then darkness claimed him, the corridor's havoc spinning away into oblivion.

Chapter 11

The dim glow of Crescent Bay's streetlights cast long shadows across the empty streets as Jeremy and Lucas approached The Tiger and the Crane. It was well past midnight, the avenues eerily silent, the usual bustle of traffic and late-night revelers absent. Each step echoed against the pavement, carrying the tension of an impossible day: Sophia's narrow escape, the ruthless pursuit by Sergei's men, and the looming weight of the diamond itself—now nestled in Jeremy's arms, its shimmering glow muffled beneath a thick cloth.

Jeremy shifted the bundle carefully, wincing at the lingering pain in his ribs where a guard's rifle had cracked into him earlier. He forced a breath, trying to quell the swirl of emotions roiling inside. The diamond was more than just a cosmic power source; it was the key to his wave grid—once letting him surf the sky as a masked vigilante. Now, it felt like a curse, drawing danger to everyone he cared about.

Lucas glanced warily at the deserted alleyways. "You sure Mr. Zhang's still awake?"

Jeremy shrugged. "He rarely sleeps more than a few hours. Probably meditating, reading, or cooking."

A small, humorless laugh escaped Lucas. "Sounds nice. I haven't had a decent meal or a moment's peace in …" He paused, shaking his head. "Feels like forever."

Reaching the restaurant's back entrance, they found the door slightly ajar, a strip of golden light spilling into the alley. With a cautious nudge, Jeremy pushed it open. A soft chime announced their arrival. Inside, the dining room was dim and empty, chairs stacked on tables. The gentle odor of ginger and cooking oil clung to the air, a last vestige of a day's work.

Behind the counter stood Mr. Zhang, wiping down a cast-iron wok with a calm, deliberate motion. He didn't look up as they entered. "Why are you here?" he asked quietly. "It's really late."

Jeremy exchanged a glance with Lucas, then stepped forward. "We … needed your advice." His voice sounded flatter than he intended, the day's exhaustion draped over every syllable.

Mr. Zhang set the wok aside, straightening. His eyes narrowed when he noticed the cloth-wrapped bundle in Jeremy's arms. "What is it you bring me?"

A knot of anxiety tightened in Jeremy's chest. He exhaled, then unwrapped the cloth, revealing the diamond's soft luminescence. The glow spilled into the restaurant, dancing over the walls in gentle waves of color.

Instantly, Mr. Zhang's posture stiffened, and he moved closer, expression turning grave.

"This …" he said, voice barely above a whisper. He stretched out a hand, stopping just shy of the gem's surface, feeling the energy radiating from it. "It resonates with immense power."

Lucas nodded, stepping forward. "That's why we're here."

Jeremy gently set the diamond on the counter, careful not to let it roll or shift. "We don't know where else to turn. We need to hide it, or … or something."

Mr. Zhang's gaze flickered between Jeremy and Lucas, then back to the diamond. "Explain from the beginning," he said. "What is this stone? And why do you come to me now, at this hour, with danger in your eyes?"

Jeremy swallowed, running a hand through his messy hair. He realized with a pang that, until this moment, he had never told Mr. Zhang the whole story—how he'd become the sky surfer or how the diamond fueled that double life. "All right," he began. "Short version. Some weeks ago, I fell into a ditch on the outskirts of town. Underground cave or something. Found this … glowing thing, felt like it was calling me. Turned out to be a diamond. Or at least, it looks like one."

Mr. Zhang lifted an eyebrow. "Calling you?"

Jeremy shrugged. "It's hard to explain. But from the moment I touched it, I felt … connected. Like it recognized me. I told Lucas about it, and we realized it wasn't just a rock. It's some insane power source. He used it to build a wave grid—energy waves that let me surf the sky, basically. I became some kind of masked vigilante. The news calls me the 'sky surfer.'"

A slight tremor passed through Mr. Zhang's features, though he kept calm. "You? The one the city whispers about?"

Lucas nodded. "He was unstoppable, for a while. Gliding across rooftops, stopping petty crimes. We thought we were doing good. But that drew attention."

"Specifically," Jeremy added, "the attention of a Russian mobster named Sergei—a real psychopath. He heard rumors of my feats and tracked the source.

Once he knew about the diamond, he wouldn't quit. He attacked our lab to steal it."

Mr. Zhang's voice dropped. "You have a lab?"

Lucas mustered a weary half smile. "I'm an inventor, engineer, and more. Or was. Now that the lab's wrecked, I'm just another guy on the run. They kidnapped Sophia—my friend—and threatened to kill us if we didn't hand over the diamond. We eventually got her back, but we barely escaped. Sergei still wants the diamond, and he won't stop until he gets it."

Jeremy exhaled shakily, hands clenching. "And more than that, Mr. Zhang—this diamond is dangerous in anyone's hands. If some government or corporation decides they want it, everything we know could change. Wars could start over it."

Mr. Zhang listened in silence, his gaze never leaving the gem's glow. At length, he let out a slow breath. "This is no mere trinket. Its energy … it's like a living creature. I sense it could consume those who abuse it."

"Exactly," Lucas said. "So that's why we're here. We have no idea where to stash it. If we keep it, Sergei's men keep coming. If we throw it in the ocean, someone might fish it out eventually. Destroying it seems impossible—it's indestructible."

Mr. Zhang reached out, letting his fingertips hover near the gem's aura. "Not a gift," he murmured, "but a burden. A heavy one. Jeremy, you realize your role as the 'sky surfer' was tied to this stone. If you hide it, you lose that power forever."

Jeremy's stomach twisted. *He's right.* He'd known it intellectually, but hearing it out loud felt like a final blow. The wave grid, the exhilaration of gliding above the city, the chance to be a hero—gone. He forced a weak nod. "I know. Honestly, part of me doesn't want to let it go. But look what it's done to our lives. We're in mortal danger, and the city could be at risk if Sergei harnesses it. I can't keep using it like a toy."

Mr. Zhang's expression softened, acknowledging the inner conflict. "To cling to power invites suffering. Perhaps the bravest act is to let it go."

A beat of silence passed, thick with unspoken tension.

"Any suggestions?" Lucas asked, voice tight with anxiety. "We can't just bury it in the backyard."

"There is a place," Mr. Zhang said softly. "A temple, far from here, in the mountains. Ancient. The monks who reside there guard objects that defy the modern world. If they accept your diamond, they will hide it beyond the reach of men like Sergei."

Lucas stared. "You know such a temple? Like an actual secret monastery?"

Mr. Zhang nodded. "Yes, I happen to know it very well."

Jeremy let out a shaky sigh. "So that's our best shot. We give it to them. Let them lock it away for good."

A faint sadness touched Mr. Zhang's eyes. "Yes. But the journey is long and perilous. You must travel far north, beyond borders, crossing harsh terrain."

Lucas swallowed. "We'll do whatever it takes."

Jeremy looked down at the diamond's gleaming surface, a swirl of mixed emotions roiling. It had saved him, let him become something more than the aimless kid he used to be. Yet it also threatened everything he cared about. "No matter the cost," he agreed quietly.

Mr. Zhang gave a slight nod. "Then be prepared. Let go of your old attachments, Jeremy."

A pang shot through Jeremy's chest, an ache not entirely physical. He pictured the rooftops at dawn, the wind in his hair, the city's lights stretching to the horizon. It was the closest thing to freedom he'd ever known. But he also saw the blood on his hands from the fortress fight, the bullets whizzing by. *Inside reflects the outside.*

He breathed through the sorrow. "I understand. Maybe this is how it was meant to be," he said, voice low. "I won't lie, I loved the thrill. But seeing how quickly it turned into chaos when bad people wanted it—I can't keep it going."

Lucas exhaled, placing a hand on Jeremy's shoulder. "You're still you, man. Diamond or not, you did a lot of good. That doesn't just vanish."

Jeremy gave a half smile, though tears threatened. "Thanks. But this is bigger than me."

Mr. Zhang let the weight of their words settle. "Then we must plan. We cannot remain in Crescent Bay. If Sergei suspects you're still here, he'll tear the city apart searching. We must leave quietly."

Mr. Zhang glanced at the clock on the wall, which read well past midnight. "We rest for a few hours, gather supplies, and depart at dawn. The sooner we vanish, the less likely Sergei can track us."

Lucas nodded. "We'll need passports. I'm guessing we already have ours, but I can whip one up for Sophia without a problem. After all, we hacked into the Department of State back when we were looking for Sergei."

Jeremy glanced over with a worried expression. "So, what do I tell my parents? Any bright ideas?"

Lucas shrugged. "Not my problem. My dad knows he messed up big-time, so he owes me. Just say you're going to some training camp."

"In China?" Jeremy asked, eyebrows raised.

"Exactly," Lucas said with a laugh. "Tell them you're going to one of those indoor surf pools. Your parents are so busy, they probably won't even question it. We'll only be gone for ten days, anyway."

Jeremy exhaled, relief flashing across his face. "You know what? That might actually work."

He swallowed, staring at the diamond's glow. The swirling lights danced on the walls, reflecting in the worn, empty restaurant. His mind flicked through memories: his first sky-surf ride at sunrise, the adrenaline of swooping between skyscrapers, the laughter with Lucas when everything seemed simple. Now he was about to bury that life in a remote temple forever. A trembling sense of loss threaded through him.

He gently wrapped the diamond back in the cloth, extinguishing its light. *I guess this is farewell*, he thought, exhaling the knot in his throat. No more bullet-slowing illusions, no more wave grid. But maybe fewer bullet wounds, fewer raging criminals, fewer innocents in danger.

In the quiet that followed, Mr. Zhang motioned them toward the back. "Rest what little you can. We leave at dawn."

Jeremy turned to follow, but paused at the threshold, looking once more at the dark silhouettes of chairs stacked on tables. This place—like his wave grid—had been a kind of refuge, a training ground for the powers the diamond granted. *That time is over*, he told himself. *Focus on saving the world from this thing.*

Lucas touched his elbow gently. "Come on," he said, voice gentle. "We'll figure the rest out as we go."

They disappeared into the hallway's gloom, the hush settling again over the restaurant. Mr. Zhang trailed behind, flipping off most of the lights. The diamond's faint glow peeked through the cloth as he carried it to a safer corner, away from prying eyes. They had precious little time to gather strength before a perilous journey, haunted by Sergei's pursuit and the knowledge that the city's sky surfer would soon exist only in memory.

Yet in that quiet moment, despite the fear of what lay ahead, Jeremy felt a pang of acceptance. *Inside reflects the outside*, he recalled. He couldn't cling to the diamond's allure, not if it threatened everyone he loved. Sometimes letting go is the only way to protect what matters.

Hours later—though it felt like mere minutes—they emerged from fitful rest. The night sky had shifted to a thin gray band of predawn light. Mr. Zhang's calm presence guided them to the alley once more, each carrying a small bag. The diamond remained cocooned in layers of cloth, the slightest glow visible. Jeremy cradled it gingerly.

Mr. Zhang surveyed the sleepy street, scanning for any sign of watchers. Satisfied, he turned to Jeremy and Lucas. "We'll take a quiet route to the airport. Once we're airborne, Sergei cannot follow easily. Then we make our way to the mountains." He hesitated, the lines on his face deepening with concern. "Are you truly ready for this?"

Chapter 12

The Beijing airport was a whirlwind of noise and motion, a gleaming maze of gates and steel, the overhead signs glowing with Mandarin characters and the English translations beneath. A constant hum of announcements rattled the air. Jeremy maneuvered his duffel bag behind him, his old skateboard strapped on top, wheels clacking with every jostle. Lucas, seated in his wheelchair, had an overnight bag balanced on his lap, his eyes darting between blinking departure boards and the press of travelers rushing past.

"This is like a giant anthill," Lucas muttered, tucking in his chin as a family wheeled a tall stack of luggage perilously close. "We're basically in a human tide here."

Jeremy offered a small grin, weaving around a knot of tourists. "Relax, I've seen worse. This is just the standard Beijing bustle."

Ahead of them, Sophia led the way, her posture confident and her expression focused. She kept an eye on Mr. Zhang, who navigated the chaos with the ease of someone long accustomed to crowds. He turned, waving them closer.

"We must keep up," he urged in a clipped tone, "or we'll miss the train."

They finally cleared customs and left the airport terminal behind, stepping into a sprawling rail station that glittered with sleek lines and polished tile floors. Towering windows threw rectangles of sunlight across high-speed bullet trains arrayed on multiple platforms.

"Now this is cool," Jeremy said, letting out a low whistle. Even as a modern city kid, the sight of the silver bullet trains—like metal arrows aimed at the horizon—made his heart flutter with excitement.

Lucas nodded, shifting his wheelchair with a neat push of his gloved hands. "Impressive tech, but let's not get distracted. We're on a clock."

Sophia smiled faintly. "Still more civilized than a Greyhound bus, right?"

They boarded one of the bullet trains, the interior hushed and spacious, seats arranged in neat rows with generous legroom. Jeremy took a seat next to a window, stowing his duffel at his feet. Lucas parked his wheelchair in a designated space near the door, locking the wheels. Mr. Zhang set a small bag of his own overhead, then sat across from them, crossing his arms in silent composure.

When the train glided from the station, the acceleration pressed them into their seats. The cityscape soon fell away, replaced by a patchwork of farmland, rivers, and distant hills. Jeremy let his tired mind drift, lulled by the train's gentle hum. He couldn't stop thinking about the diamond, currently bundled in Lucas's backpack, hidden under spare clothes. So far, there was no sign that Sergei's men had followed, yet he couldn't shake the feeling of being hunted.

The bullet train devoured kilometers at incredible speed, Chinese countryside morphing into a long mural of fields and scattered villages. Occasionally, they'd pass smaller towns, stations, or industrial zones. Lucas alternated between peering out the window and tapping on a small laptop plugged into a portable battery. Sophia gazed at the scenery, while Mr. Zhang sipped tea from a paper cup, eyes half closed as though meditating.

Eventually, the overhead speakers chimed, announcing their approach to a northern hub. Jeremy stretched, eyes flicking to Mr. Zhang. "So this is where we catch another train?"

Mr. Zhang shook his head. "We'll hire a driver next. The mountains are not easily reached by rail."

Sophia sighed, a mixture of anticipation and wariness crossing her face. "And after that, the temple?"

"Precisely," Mr. Zhang confirmed. "Prepare yourselves."

Lucas closed his laptop, rubbing the back of his neck. "We're halfway across the world from Crescent Bay, and it still doesn't feel far enough from Sergei."

Jeremy gave a faint nod. The thought of Sergei or his henchmen showing up in these remote places unsettled him. *But better here than somewhere the diamond could be easily stolen.*

They disembarked at a smaller station, where a sober-faced driver Mr. Zhang had arranged met them with a sturdy SUV. The man greeted them politely, loading their bags with stoic efficiency. Mr. Zhang spoke quietly with him in Mandarin for a few minutes before they set off on winding roads that rose steadily into the hills. The engine rumbled as they left the bustle of the city behind, climbing through wooded valleys and terraced fields.

Jeremy peered out at the passing landscape—old villages, misty mountainsides, the occasional tangle of bamboo. The air grew cooler, crisper. Part of him relaxed, as though the natural beauty promised safety. Yet a small knot in his gut remained, a silent dread that Sergei might appear at any turn.

Lucas adjusted his wheelchair so he could look out a side window. "You okay, man?" he asked Jeremy quietly. "You seem … distant."

Jeremy shrugged. "Just thinking about all of it." He wanted to say more about how the diamond used to define him, how he once soared above Crescent Bay as the sky surfer, but he didn't want to dwell. "We're doing the right thing," he said at last.

"Yeah." Lucas looked unconvinced but didn't press.

Their driver eventually halted at a remote outpost—a narrow trailhead marked by an ancient archway carved with faded Chinese characters. The sign overhead read something about an old monastery. The driver refused to go further, gesturing at the rocky footpath that snaked upward. Mr. Zhang thanked him, settling payment.

Sophia slid out, helping Lucas with a portable ramp so he could guide his wheelchair onto the rocky ground. Mr. Zhang strapped on a small pack. Jeremy hefted his own gear, skateboard clattering awkwardly. Then, with the driver's SUV rumbling back down the road, they faced the steep ascent alone.

Mr. Zhang quietly took the lead. The path climbed through pine forests, patches of bamboo, and occasional stone shrines. Lichen and moss clung to weathered statues of warrior monks, their features eroded by centuries of rain. The hush felt profound—only their footsteps, a few chirping birds, and the soft whir of Lucas's motorized wheelchair as he navigated carefully over rough spots were heard.

Sophia walked beside Lucas, offering a steadying hand whenever the path narrowed or stepped up sharply. Mr. Zhang sometimes scouted ahead, ensuring they wouldn't encounter impassable terrain. Jeremy followed, eyes scanning for any sign of watchers. None, at least for now. The slow pace gave him time to reflect. This was the mission: hide the diamond. Save the world from its destructive potential. No talk of wave grids or bullet-stopping shows of power.

After hours of exhausting climb, they reached a plateau. Jeremy swallowed hard, chest burning from the altitude. In the distance, a cluster of ancient buildings spread across a ridge—elegant stone walls, curved roofs with intricate carvings, prayer flags dancing in the breeze. Soft chanting drifted through the mountain air like a faint lullaby. Lucas gazed up with silent awe, the wheelchair's motor quiet now as they paused to admire the view.

"Welcome," Mr. Zhang said, gesturing at the temple gates. "These monks keep to themselves, rarely venturing beyond these mountains. If they accept the diamond, it may remain hidden forever."

An imposing gate opened to a courtyard paved with worn cobblestones. Monks in saffron robes glided quietly between halls, some pausing to eye the newcomers with curiosity. Approaching them was a tall figure in similar robes. He grinned widely at Mr. Zhang, speaking in rapid Mandarin, his voice resonating with warmth. They exchanged a quick embrace.

"Brother." The older man greeted him in English, his words flowing seamlessly after a rapid exchange in Chinese. "At last, you've returned, and with guests." He offered a respectful bow to Lucas, Sophia, and Jeremy. "Welcome to our sanctuary."

Mr. Zhang bowed low in return. "Thank you for welcoming us, my brother. Master Zhang, I've missed you greatly."

Jeremy's eyebrows shot up. "Wait—you two are actually brothers? I had no idea you even had a brother, Mr. Zhang."

Mr. Zhang smiled, a hint of amusement in his eyes. "That's because you never thought to ask."

"I sense you carry a great burden, brother," Master Zhang said.

Mr. Zhang said quietly, "Yes, brother. We must speak privately."

The older monk nodded, guiding them deeper into the temple. They passed tranquil courtyards filled with trees, ponds shimmering under lantern light, and intricately carved stone pillars that soared into the sky. Jeremy felt a hush descend, as though the very air demanded reverence. A pang gripped his chest. *This is where we leave the diamond.*

They were led into a low-ceilinged corridor lit by lanterns. The scent of incense mingled with centuries-old dust. Stone steps descended into a vault-like chamber carved from the mountain's bedrock. Shelves and niches in the walls held relics wrapped in silk, glints of precious metals, and ancient scrolls. Echoes of whispered prayers drifted from hidden corners.

Master Zhang came to a stop in front of a massive wooden door reinforced with iron. Turning to Mr. Zhang and the others, he said, "This is our secret repository—where we keep artifacts that must never be allowed into the outside world again."

He pushed the door open, revealing a dimly lit chamber packed with ancient Chinese scrolls, dusty spell books, carved statues, gleaming weapons, and rare stones. As they stepped inside, Master Zhang guided them from one artifact to the next, explaining the history and power behind each.

"You see," he began, addressing the group, "humanity has always raced to acquire the most powerful tools and weapons, constantly trying to tip the balance of power in their favor. It wasn't long before our ancestors realized how dangerous that could be. So they built this temple and chose monks—those who can rise above ego and think of the greater good—to guard these treasures."

Lucas, eyes wide, suddenly pointed to a beautiful sword displayed behind glass. "What's that?"

Master Zhang followed his gaze. "That is the emperor's secret sword. Legend says that if the chosen person wields it, they can summon the Sky Dragon and command it. Of course, if this power ever fell into the wrong hands, it would spell disaster."

Lucas inhaled, adjusting the wheelchair's position. "I guess this is where the diamond belongs."

Sophia set a hand on the bag containing the diamond, nodding. "Yes."

With deft motions, Master Zhang unlocked a series of metal bars and slid the door open, revealing a small, torchlit room. A single pedestal of polished stone sat at the center. Mr. Zhang gestured to Jeremy, who carefully withdrew the diamond from Lucas's pack. Its glow lit the walls in ghostly blues and greens, bright enough to make them squint.

For a moment, Jeremy stared into its depths. *This is it*, he thought. *No turning back.* He recalled the bullet-slowing illusions, the thrill of unstoppable motion, the times he'd soared over Crescent Bay's skyline. Now, that power would be entombed here, out of reach. A slow ache coiled in his chest. But he forced himself to step forward.

He placed the diamond gently on the stone pedestal. Master Zhang moved around it, sprinkling fine powder that shimmered in the flickering light. A hush fell over the room, as though even the stone walls held their breath. Then Master Zhang sealed a glass dome over the gem, locking it with a set of archaic keys, each turn echoing finality.

"Here, it shall remain. We vow no outsider shall learn of it, or wield it," said Master Zhang quietly.

***

They stayed on in the temple for a few days, adjusting to the high altitude and participating in modest temple chores. The monks greeted them politely but offered little conversation. Jeremy found it oddly soothing. No more frantic chases, no surge of the diamond's power. At times, though, he'd glance at the sealed vault door and feel a hollow pang. *We did the right thing. If we don't hide it, people die.*

By day, they helped gather firewood, cleaned courtyards, or listened to the monks chanting in the main hall. By night, they slept in sparse dormitories, lulled by the mountain wind. The tension in Jeremy's shoulders eased day by day, though he occasionally caught Mr. Zhang eyeing the horizon warily. No sign of Sergei. Maybe they'd truly outrun him.

***

On the fifth morning of their stay at the temple, an eerie rumbling shattered the predawn stillness. Jeremy jolted upright, heart hammering against his ribs. He blinked away sleep and scrambled outside, where he found Mr. Zhang and Lucas on a stone balcony overlooking the surrounding peaks.

Thick, inky smoke curled into the sky from one of the nearby mountains. It glowed an unsettling orange, and as the rising sun illuminated the horizon, they could see molten rock spilling down the rugged slope in torrents.

Sophia appeared, her hair still messy from sleep. She stared wide-eyed at the churning lava. "Is that … Are we looking at an actual volcano?" she asked, her voice trembling.

Mr. Zhang pressed his lips into a thin line. "A dormant crater, now awakened."

A chorus of startled shouts echoed in the temple's courtyard below. Monks hurried along the walkways, pointing toward the inferno. Far down the mountain, a small village lay directly in the path of the lava flow. Flickers of panic ran through Jeremy's veins as he imagined the devastation about to unfold.

Lucas gripped the rims of his wheelchair until his knuckles turned white. "If we don't do something, people will die. We can't stand by and watch."

Sophia hesitated, shooting a worried glance back toward the vault. "But the diamond's locked away. Using it could tip off Sergei to our location. Is it worth the risk?"

Jeremy squared his shoulders. "We don't have a choice. People's lives are at stake. We help them—no question. Sophia, get the diamond. Lucas, fire up your computer and activate the grid. I'll suit up."

They rushed into action. Lucas hurried to a secluded chamber to power up the high-tech system they'd brought with them, tapping frantically at his keyboard as streams of code lit up the screen. Sophia sprinted to the vault, heart pounding, and retrieved the diamond. It glimmered with an unearthly light, as though it, too, sensed the crisis unfolding outside.

Within minutes, they reassembled near the courtyard. The grid—a series of pulsing energy lines that could be manipulated into different shapes—hummed with power. Jeremy, now equipped with the specialized suit, stepped onto the custom surfboard that Lucas had integrated with the grid's energy. His eyes narrowed with determination.

"Go time," Lucas said, voice cracking with adrenaline and urgency.

"Let's do this," Jeremy replied, leaning forward. In a flash, the energy grid propelled him downward, weaving through the temple's terraces and over jagged outcroppings toward the endangered village.

Lucas's voice crackled through Jeremy's earpiece, the diamond-empowered tech linking them all. "I see a mother and child trapped to your right. The roof of their house just collapsed—get them out!"

Jeremy jerked the board to the right, threading through a narrow alley. Heat blasted his face as he dodged scorching embers carried on the wind. He spotted the mother and child huddled beneath a crumbling awning. In one swift motion, he scooped them onto the board, barely avoiding a massive tree trunk collapsing in a burst of flame behind them.

"You're clear!" Lucas shouted.

Jeremy's pulse pounded in his ears. He rushed the family to higher ground, setting them down near a cluster of monks already guiding villagers to safety.

"Another family, two houses over!" Lucas's voice cut in. "Lava's about to reach them!"

Jeremy glanced toward the blazing hillside. Molten rock glowed with ferocious heat as it advanced with terrifying speed. He clenched his fists and activated two micro-missiles from the bracelet that Lucas had engineered. They soared through the air, striking the ground just ahead of the lava. The blast created a deep fissure, channeling the flow away from the family's home. The family scrambled out the back door, half lifting, half dragging each other as they fled to safety.

"Nice!" Lucas called, relief evident in his tone.

But there was no time to celebrate. Jeremy guided his energy board around fallen timbers and blazing debris, helping anyone he saw pinned or trapped. With each rescue, his muscles burned and sweat stung his eyes, but the fear and determination in every villager's face pushed him forward.

The lava crept closer, swallowing streets and setting trees ablaze. Yet with the combined efforts of the monks, villagers, and Jeremy's diamond-fueled gear, people found routes to higher ground. Screams and the roar of the volcano merged into a chaotic chorus that spurred him on.

Finally, after what felt like an eternity, the tide of scorching molten rock slowed. The last pockets of trapped villagers emerged, guided by temple monks and flanked by Mr. Zhang and Sophia, who had descended to help with first aid. The air smelled of ash and smoke, and Jeremy's lungs burned with every breath, but he remained on high alert, scanning the area for any sign of survivors.

When the villagers were safe and the lava's fury began to subside, Jeremy glided back toward Lucas. He hopped off the board, collapsing to his knees from sheer exhaustion.

Lucas reached out, placing a hand on Jeremy's shoulder. "You did it," he said quietly.

Jeremy exhaled a shaky breath, adrenaline still pumping. He glanced over at the saved villagers, now hugging their children and thanking the monks. Gratitude and relief mingled with worry over whether Sergei might now sense the diamond's power.

But one thing was sure: they'd made the right call. Lives had been saved—and for Jeremy, Sophia, Lucas, and Mr. Zhang, that was worth any risk.

Chapter 13

The mountain air had finally grown cool again, a delicate hush settling over the high-perched temple after the day's frantic rescue efforts. Overhead, the sky was ink-black and scattered with vivid stars. In the courtyard, Jeremy and Lucas sat on a crumbled stone step, still catching their breath. Sophia lingered nearby, arms looped around her knees, her gaze distant as though half expecting more calamities. An occasional swirl of wind carried the faint aroma of incense from deep within the ancient complex.

At Lucas's side, a small diamond-powered setup hummed—a rig he'd cobbled together from leftover gear. He tapped on a laptop perched on his wheelchair's arm, scanning residual signals in the region. "Energy fluctuations ... minimal," he muttered, adjusting a dial.

Sophia glanced over at him. "So, no sign of an immediate threat?"

"Seems quiet," Lucas replied, exhaling a shaky sigh. "But quiet can be deceiving."

Jeremy leaned back, pressing a hand to the bruises on his ribs. "We might get a break. The day's been too insane." He paused. "Still, we have to stay alert."

Sophia nodded, voice hushed. "I just hope we can keep this place safe a while."

The temple soared around them in shadowy grandeur: towering rooftops, carved eaves, and intricate gold trim depicting phoenixes and dragons. In the darkness, the buildings seemed ethereal, as though existing outside of time. Yet beneath that serene facade lay tension, a sense that they'd survived one crisis, but more could follow.

A low, distant thrum echoed across the mountains, halting their idle chatter. Jeremy bolted upright, instincts screaming. "Do you hear that?"

Lucas's eyes flicked upward. "That's not temple bells, is it?"

Jeremy's expression darkened. "Helicopters. They found us."

Sophia inhaled sharply. "Oh no."

The faint rotor noise swelled into a deafening roar as multiple helicopters materialized against the moonlit horizon—dark silhouettes with searchlights flicking on. Muzzle flashes erupted from the lead chopper, sparking in the night. Bullets raked across the outer temple walls, blasting centuries-old stone into clouds of dust.

"They're firing!" Sophia shouted, ducking behind a fallen column. Stone chips pelted the courtyard, each impact echoing like thunder among the winding corridors.

Jeremy pivoted, yelling, "Inside, everyone!" He grabbed the handles of Lucas's wheelchair, pushing him toward the nearest corridor. Sophia scrambled behind them, hair flying as more bullets whizzed overhead, smashing statues and carved railings.

But the temple's monks refused to cower. Led by Master Zhang in gold-trimmed robes, they swiftly positioned themselves in the courtyard, unwavering eyes reflecting torchlight. Mr. Zhang—Jeremy's teacher—stood at his brother's side, every muscle coiled with readiness.

"Defend the temple!" Master Zhang roared in Mandarin, staff raised. Monks rushed forward, forming a perimeter near the courtyard's central statue of Bodhidharma.

From the helicopters, multiple ropes dropped, and Sergei's mercenaries descended, clad in black tactical gear with assault rifles. Their boots hit the courtyard flagstones in harsh thuds, voices barking commands in thick Russian accents.

"Secure the area!" one soldier snarled, scanning for targets with night-vision goggles.

Then, a second helicopter swooped in, depositing the imposing figure of Sergei himself—tall, broad-shouldered, eyes gleaming with cold intent. He surveyed the temple's ancient pillars and wounded walls, a sneer twisting his lips. "We end this now," he hissed.

***

Gunshots erupted in a furious cacophony. The monks lunged in perfect unison, bridging centuries of martial tradition to face modern firearms. A monk spun low, sweeping a soldier's legs from under him before disarming the weapon with a lightning hand strike. Another deflected a rifle butt swing using only his forearm, then delivered a spinning kick to the attacker's chest, sending him crashing into the nearest pillar.

Saffron robes swirled in the chaotic glow of muzzle flashes. One mercenary hurled a grenade, but a monk seized it in mid-arc, pivoted on a single foot, and heaved it back with uncanny precision. It detonated among the mercenaries' own ranks, showering the flagstones with shrapnel and screams. Smoke billowed, obscuring the courtyard's carved statues.

Master and Mr. Zhang fought side by side like twin hurricanes unleashed. Master Zhang wielded a tall staff, weaving it through rifle barrels and delivering punishing strikes to chins, ribs, or knees; Mr. Zhang fought with a blend of open-palmed attacks and lightning kicks, each blow crackling with fierce discipline.

At one point, Master Zhang cracked a soldier's arm, forcing him to drop his submachine gun. Smirking at his brother, he teased, "I see cooking noodles in America made you soft, brother."

Mr. Zhang dodged a hail of bullets, hooking his staff around another soldier's weapon, yanking it aside. He tossed a cocky grin back. "Or maybe it just made me more refined."

They both lunged at once, staff and fist colliding with an unfortunate pair of mercenaries, sending them sprawling across shattered stone. The synergy between the brothers was awe-inspiring, a fluid blend of skill and banter that defied the modern weapons arrayed against them.

Near the temple entrance, Jeremy refused to hide. He'd practiced long hours under Mr. Zhang's tutelage and now put it to use. Racing forward, he shoulder-checked a soldier who threatened a wounded monk, grappling the man's rifle and twisting it free. A second soldier leaped in with a knife, but Jeremy ducked, landing a swift kick to the side. The soldier collapsed with a pained grunt.

More ropes dropped from the hovering gunships, depositing fresh waves of soldiers. Rockets screeched overhead, slamming into the temple's upper halls. Entire sections of the roof caved in, centuries-old beams splitting like matchsticks. A crescendo of dust and flame consumed the night air.

Despite the monks' incredible prowess, the relentless flood of mercenaries slowly wore them down. Soldiers pinned them from multiple angles. A bullet clipped Master Zhang's staff, splintering its tip. Mr. Zhang staggered from a close-range shot that grazed his shoulder, blood staining his torn sleeve. Monks fell under superior firepower, their saffron robes smudged with grime and blood.

Sergei prowled closer, weaving among the chaos. His submachine gun spat short bursts, forcing the wounded or cornered monks to retreat. The courtyard reeked of gunpowder, shattered stone, and spilled incense braziers. Embers glowed in pockets of rubble. Gritting his teeth, Jeremy engaged two mercenaries near a half-collapsed column, disarming one with a wrist lock and flipping him onto broken tiles. But a third soldier blindsided him with a rifle butt to the ribs. Jeremy let out a sharp hiss of pain, rolling with the blow.

A wave of bullets forced Mr. Zhang and his brother to take cover behind a chunk of fallen rooftop. Sergei, spotting an opening, advanced deeper into the courtyard. That's when he noticed Sophia behind a broken pillar, breathing hard from exhaustion.

With ruthless speed, Sergei lunged, yanking Sophia upright, pressing a pistol to her temple. She cried out, her legs kicking. "Stop!" she pleaded, panic etched on her face.

"Drop your weapons!" Sergei roared, voice booming over the gunshots. "Or I blow her brains out!"

A hush fell, broken only by the crackle of distant fires. The monks, battered but still standing, froze. Mr. Zhang cursed under his breath, eyes darting for a rescue angle. Jeremy stood rigid, fists clenched, chest heaving.

"You can't stop me now." Sergei's grin was cruel, pressing the barrel harder against Sophia's head. "Hand over the diamond. Where is it?"

"I … We can figure something out. Just don't hurt her!" Jeremy yelled, voice raw with desperation.

Before Sergei could respond, an ear-splitting roar tore through the night. The battered rooftop overhead exploded in a shower of ancient timbers, dust, and sparks. Soldiers ducked, shouting in alarm. From the swirling debris, a vast serpentine figure descended—a Chinese dragon, sinuous body shimmering with emerald and gold scales in the moonlight. Twin horns curved from its majestic head, whiskers trailing elegantly, and a whiskered muzzle parted to reveal razor-sharp teeth. Its elongated form twisted with fluid grace, clawed limbs bracing its sinuous body midair. A fiery glow pulsed in its throat.

Everyone—even Sergei—gaped in disbelief. "What the hell …?" he stammered, reflexively releasing Sophia, who darted away.

With an earth-shaking roar, the dragon exhaled a jet of flame. A helicopter hovering above them was instantly consumed in a raging inferno, metal fragments raining on the courtyard in arcs of molten steel. Soldiers screamed, dropping weapons, some running for the ropes, others firing wildly at the mythical beast. Bullets pinged off the dragon's plated scales, leaving no mark.

The monks seized the moment. Master Zhang clutched a broken staff, Mr. Zhang swirling a recovered short sword. They rejoined the fight with renewed vigor. Jeremy dashed to help a wounded comrade, scanning for Lucas. He found him near a chunk of statue, wheelchair braced, the emperor's sword in his hand, its jade inlays shining eerily bright.

"You have the *sword*?" Jeremy shouted over the dragon's thunderous roar.

Lucas flashed a triumphant grin. "I saw the old texts referencing it. Guess it still works if you know the right codes," he said, tapping the hilt's carved Chinese characters. "We needed major backup."

Sophia gasped, eyes fixed on the colossal beast swirling above them. "That's a real Chinese dragon?!"

"It's real enough," Lucas replied, brandishing the sword. The dragon, as if guided by his summons, unleashed another torrent of fire, incinerating a second helicopter. Flaming wreckage scattered across the temple courtyard, forcing mercenaries to dive aside. Some attempted to flee into the labyrinth of halls, only to be intercepted by monks or pinned under falling debris.

"Retreat!" an officer yelled, voice breaking with terror. "Retreat, or that monster kills us all!"

Sergei, still reeling, made a desperate dash for the last helicopter. The pilot hovered precariously, scanning for a safe landing zone amid the carnage. But the dragon swooped down in a serpent-like arc, whiskered muzzle opening in a bellow that shook the temple pillars. One claw smashed through the chopper's rotor, metal shrieking. The helicopter spun out of control, exploding in a spectacular fireball that lit the courtyard like a second sunrise.

With that final helicopter reduced to smoldering wreckage, the courtyard fell strangely silent, aside from the crackle of flames and the moans of the wounded. The Chinese dragon settled onto the ground, coils draping elegantly across shattered columns. Its whiskers waved gently in the cool night breeze, luminous eyes surveying the scorched battlefield as though half curious, half satisfied.

All around, soldiers lay scattered—some lifeless, others too shell-shocked to fight. Monks regrouped near the battered walls, assisting the injured or bowing in reverence to the dragon that had come to their rescue. Smoke drifted across the complex, illuminated by torches and occasional bursts of flame from the wrecked aircraft. Sergei was nowhere in sight—presumably lost in the final explosion or fled in the confusion.

Jeremy exhaled in relief, adrenaline draining from his body in waves. *It's over. At least for now.*

Lucas maneuvered his wheelchair forward, the emperor's sword balanced across his lap, cautious to approach the resting dragon. The creature turned its horned head, meeting Lucas's gaze with an almost regal curiosity. An unspoken connection seemed to pass between them—man and myth, bound by the sword's ancient power.

Jeremy limped across the rubble, hooking an arm under Mr. Zhang's shoulder to help him stand. The older man's robe was torn and bloodied, but he flashed Jeremy a hard-won smile. "That was quite a show," Mr. Zhang murmured.

"You fought well, Chef!" came a teasing voice behind them. Master Zhang, bruised and cut, approached with a half smile, staff still clutched in one hand.

Mr. Zhang chuckled through the pain. "I do miss my quiet kitchen and noodles."

Sophia joined them, breath ragged but eyes bright with relief. "Thank God. We actually survived."

Chapter 14

The temple was a mere shadow of its former glory. Days after Sergei's ruthless assault and the awe-inspiring arrival of the Chinese dragon, thin tendrils of smoke still curled skyward from scorched timbers and shattered rooftops. Stone columns, once carved with centuries-old images of monks and ancient deities, now lay cracked and strewn across the courtyard. Even so, the mountain air retained an odd sense of serenity, as though these sacred walls refused to surrender to despair.

Amid the quiet bustle, monks moved tirelessly, nursing the wounded, salvaging relics from the debris, and working to shore up dangerously weakened arches. Sunlight spilled over the high peaks, illuminating dust motes drifting through the corridors of the battered complex. Despite everything, the temple felt determined to endure.

Jeremy sat cross-legged near the central courtyard, an uneven patch of ground that had become both a makeshift triage area and a place for solemn reflection. The air carried the lingering tang of burnt incense mixed with the faint metallic smell of old blood. In front of him, resting on a soft swatch of silk, lay the diamond— its opalescent glow pulsing gently, as though timed to his breathing.

He couldn't tear his gaze from it. Even after all they had endured—fighting Sergei's mercenaries, summoning a dragon out of legend—the diamond's power still mystified him. He sensed it humming in his mind, a silent presence both alien and familiar. Was it alive? The question tugged at him, but no easy answers came.

A light whir accompanied Lucas as he wheeled closer in his motorized chair, the ground still littered with small stones and broken tiles. He gave Jeremy a wry grin. "You've been staring at that thing for an hour. Any chance it'll grow arms and rebuild the temple for us?"

Jeremy let out a soft snort, eyes still locked on the gem. "Tempting thought. Part of me wonders if we'd all be better off if it just ... vanished."

From a short distance away, Sophia approached. She settled beside Jeremy, arms looped around her knees. "We might not be alive if it vanished," she said quietly. "It saved us. Twice."

He exhaled, a hint of bitterness creeping into his voice. "And painted a giant target on our backs. Sergei came for it with a small army. If not for that monstrous, wonderful dragon, we'd be captured or dead."

Lucas placed his elbows on the wheelchair's armrests, expression somber. "True, but we can't deny it's helped. The eruption rescue, cracking the codes for the emperor's sword, the final stand against Sergie... The diamond's power is a double-edged sword."

Before anyone could add more, a gentle stirring of fabric announced the arrival of Mr. Zhang and his brother. Their robes were patched in places, and faint bruises lingered on their arms and faces, but they moved with a steady assurance. Master Zhang carried an ancient scroll, edges frayed and stained by time. Golden threads held the parchment together, glinting faintly whenever the diamond's glow caught them.

"You all fought bravely," Mr. Zhang said, voice calm yet resonant. "But what happened here shows that I have been entirely mistaken about one thing: simply hiding the diamond will not suffice."

Jeremy snapped his head up, confusion etched on his features. "What do you mean? We just forced Sergei to flee. The dragon sealed that deal."

Master Zhang's stern gaze swept the courtyard, pausing on the broken relics and scorched columns. "Sergei found us once. Others will as well. The diamond's power is like a beacon in a chaotic world. No matter how remote a hideout or how fortified our defenses, those who hunger for it will come."

Lucas frowned, adjusting the laptop resting on his lap. "So your plan is … what, exactly? Hand it over? That's not an option."

"Of course not," Mr. Zhang said. "But there is another path. One the temple's archives hinted at for centuries."

Master Zhang unrolled the scroll, careful not to tear the fragile edges. Its surface glowed faintly under the diamond's radiance, revealing graceful illustrations and lines of flowing script in archaic Chinese. "We discovered this after the battle, sealed in a hidden alcove. It speaks of a prophecy—an ancient tale passed from generation to generation among the monks."

A hush settled around them. Nearby monks, busy stacking fragments of wall and collecting scattered relics, paused to watch. Their eyes glimmered with curiosity at the scroll Master Zhang held in his hands.

Master Zhang began reading, voice reverent:

"From the heavens, a stone of great power shall fall. Its light shall bring balance to the world, but only in the hands of those chosen to protect it. They shall come together by fate, bound to the stone and its purpose. Through them, balance will be restored—not by the stone itself, but by the choices and actions of its guardians."

He finished and glanced up. Jeremy, Lucas, and Sophia exchanged stunned looks. The diamond's glow seemed to intensify for an instant, pulsing like a heartbeat.

"Wait," Jeremy murmured. "That's describing … us?"

Sophia brushed dust from her clothes, voice hushed. "It can't be a coincidence. Everything that happened— Sergei, the attacks, the dragon. Like some cosmic puzzle we fit into."

Lucas's expression wavered between skepticism and fascination. "It's an old legend, sure, but you can't seriously think it predicted we'd end up with this thing."

Master Zhang's brow furrowed gently. "The emperor's sword was also a legend, until you used it to bring forth the dragon. Many legends begin in truth."

Mr. Zhang folded his arms. "If the temple's records are correct, the diamond fell from the sky eons ago. Now, fate has led you to it. You have touched it, Jeremy, harnessed its power. It resonates with you—and with those who stand at your side."

Sophia let out a shaky breath. "So we're 'chosen' protectors. Great. And we thought fighting Sergei was stressful."

Jeremy ran a hand through his hair, gaze flicking between the glowing stone and the intricate calligraphy on the scroll. "If that's the case, if we're some sort of guardians, what exactly does that mean? Do we stand around waiting for more bad guys? Keep the diamond locked up somewhere? Keep summoning dragons whenever the world's in peril?"

A slight smile curved across Master Zhang's face, though sorrow still underpinned his eyes. "The prophecy does not speak of constant warfare. It speaks of balance. The diamond amplifies the actions of those it bonds with. If your hearts are pure, it can bring light and peace. If someone twisted obtains it, only darkness follows."

Mr. Zhang nodded solemnly. "Balance is not merely about big battles. It's about daily choices, big and small, that shape the world. That is the path of the chosen protectors."

Jeremy studied the diamond's glow once more, remembering the moment he first touched it in that underground cavern, how it seemed to call out to him. He'd used it to surf the sky, rescue innocents, and fend off mercenaries. But with each triumph came a new wave of trouble. "So if we accept this prophecy," he said quietly, "we can't just walk away from the diamond. We have to be part of it, part of this bigger purpose."

Master Zhang gave a measured nod. "Yes. If you refuse, the diamond's power will eventually find others, possibly those with far darker intentions."

An uneasy silence fell. In the background, the wounded moaned softly, and the battered temple groaned under its structural wounds. Jeremy inhaled the cool mountain breeze, letting it quell the swirl in his mind. *Part of me just wants a normal life, but ... can I ignore what we've done, what we can still do?*

Sophia placed a gentle hand on Jeremy's shoulder. "We've saved lives, Jer. Maybe ... maybe we're meant to save more."

Lucas tapped the side of the emperor's sword—resting against his wheelchair—almost absentmindedly. "I guess. And hey, if it means fewer Sergei-like creeps running around, I'm in."

Mr. Zhang angled his head. "Your hearts are aligned, it seems. So your next step is acceptance."

Jeremy exhaled. "Yeah. I'm in. The diamond's chosen me, or us ... Might as well see this through."

A flicker of warmth spread through the diamond's glow, as though acknowledging his words. Master Zhang rolled up the scroll with reverent care. "The stone is not a burden alone; it is also a guiding light. But it demands courage, compassion, and wisdom."

Lucas adjusted his wheelchair's position, careful not to bump the diamond's silk covering. "We're a ragtag team, but we'll do our best."

Mr. Zhang glanced around the broken courtyard. "And do not forget, the temple stands with you. We owe you a debt for helping us fend off Sergei's men. Our knowledge, relics, and skill are at your disposal."

Sophia brushed hair from her face, eyes flicking to the fallen pillars. "We'll help you rebuild, too. That's part of restoring balance, right?"

Master Zhang bowed slightly, gratitude evident. "Indeed."

For a moment, they let the gravity of the prophecy settle in. Monks drifted by, offering silent nods of respect to the group that had saved the temple from total devastation. Some paused to examine the diamond in awe, but did not linger, aware that time was needed for the wounded to heal and for repairs to begin.

Jeremy pressed a hand to his ribs, wincing at the bruises from the fight. "We can handle tough enemies, but manual labor might be a different story," he joked, earning a small laugh from Lucas.

Sophia stood, stretching her legs. "Well, if we're the chosen protectors, maybe we should start by protecting what's left of this place from the next threat—like the roof caving in on people's heads."

Lucas half smiled. "You mean physically shoring up beams and rebuilding walls? That's one battle we can fight right now."

Mr. Zhang's expression turned fond. "Balance is not all about world-shaking events. Sometimes, it's hammered out stone by stone. Let's begin."

And so, the chosen protectors—Jeremy, Sophia, and Lucas, with help from Mr. Zhang and Master Zhang—spent the next hours and days helping the temple's community. They cleared debris from the main courtyard, stacking rubble away from pathways. The monks guided them in reinforcing partially collapsed pillars with wooden braces. Over time, the temple's interior corridors began to look less like a war zone and more like a place of healing, albeit scarred by bullet holes and charred beams.

Jeremy discovered that the diamond could subtly infuse him with strength if he focused on it. Hauling heavy stones felt easier, though he tried not to overuse the gem. The prophecy hammered home the point:

their daily actions, done with compassion, shaped the diamond's role in the world. Small acts of kindness or rebuilding held as much significance as any grand battle.

Lucas adapted the diamond's energy for simpler tasks—powering basic lifts or providing temporary lighting in darkened halls. Mr. and Master Zhang occasionally remarked on how the diamond's aura seemed gentler, as though it recognized the calmer purpose. No swirling illusions of dragons or unstoppable bullet-time feats—just subtle assistance.

Sophia oversaw triage for the monks with deeper injuries, dispensing supplies from a battered medical kit that had survived the assault. She coordinated with Mr. Zhang to gather herbs from the temple's hillside garden, blending them into salves for burns and bruises.

In these quiet tasks, a sense of unity blossomed among them, forging trust that went beyond mere alliances.

***

One twilight evening, as the sky flared orange beyond the mountains, Jeremy sat on a half-repaired terrace alongside Lucas and Sophia. The diamond lay between them on a small wooden stand, flickering with subdued luminescence. Mr. Zhang and his brother were speaking softly in the background, presumably about architectural repairs and remaining mercenary threats.

"So," Sophia began, voice low, "this is us: guardians of a cosmic gem with the power to raise dragons and who knows what else."

Lucas let a soft laugh slip. "We're basically living in a fantasy novel. Though I guess that was proven the second we actually had a dragon show up."

Jeremy gazed at the temple roofs—some newly patched, others still gaping. "If what the prophecy says is true, the diamond amplifies us. But it also tests us. We can't just use it for personal gain or to nuke every villain that appears. We've gotta find that balance."

Sophia nodded. "And each day we have to choose. Are we doing this for good, or are we letting fear or anger drive us?"

Lucas fiddled with the diamond's carrying cloth. "Well, we've already done a lot of good, even if it drew trouble. If the world needs us, at least we're not alone, right?"

A warm breeze stirred the silk, making the diamond's glow dance over the terrace floor. Jeremy felt a surge of quiet resolve. "We face it together. We're chosen protectors … Guess we better live up to the name."

Night fully settled, and the final rays of sun receded beyond distant ridges. The temple's newly lit lanterns flickered along the pathways, illuminating exhausted monks heading to rest. Broken relics and half-toppled statues formed silhouettes in the gloom. The hush of the mountains returned, only the chirp of night insects and the soft chanting of a few persevering monks echoing under the stars.

At last, the Zhang brothers joined them again, faint smiles ghosting their faces.

Master Zhang lowered himself onto the terrace steps with a sigh. "Repairs continue. The monks' spirits are strong, thanks to your efforts."

Mr. Zhang inclined his head. "It's good you are settling into your role. The diamond no longer looms as a mere destructive prize. You have a purpose beyond that."

Jeremy cast his gaze on the gem, recalling the prophecy's lines: *The diamond's light only brings balance through the guardians' actions.* He took a deep breath. "We'll keep doing what's right—big or small. That's how we honor this stone's power."

Sophia's quiet voice carried a note of determination. "We can't promise perfection, but we'll try."

Lucas glanced at the ancient scroll Master Zhang had set aside. "One day at a time, right?"

Master Zhang nodded. "Yes. And if your choices remain guided by compassion, the stone shall remain a force for good."

Mr. Zhang laid a hand gently on Jeremy's shoulder. "Remember: you're not alone. The temple stands behind you, and each of you stands beside the other."

At the break of dawn, the temple stirred with renewed purpose. Monks rose early, continuing repairs to collapsed archways or starting daily chants in the less damaged halls. The chosen protectors joined them, each taking on tasks that fit their strengths: from cleaning the courtyard of debris to reassembling battered shrines.

While clearing rubble near the courtyard's perimeter, Jeremy paused to watch the sunrise bathe the mountains in pink and gold. The diamond, nestled in a small pouch at his side, glowed softly. He felt it respond to the morning's light, resonating with an undercurrent of hope. *It's no longer just a burden*, he realized. *It's a part of us, a shared destiny we accepted.*

Lucas, rummaging through the remains of the temple's library, found manuscripts that described other relics—ones connected to the emperor's sword and possibly other mythical creatures. He planned to decode them in the evenings, driven by curiosity. Sophia assisted monks in the herb garden, learning to craft medicinal balms that soothed battered muscles. The synergy of small acts—balance in daily choices—quietly took root.

***

In the afternoon, the group gathered again in the central courtyard, where the worst of the rubble had been cleared. The sun's warmth cascaded onto fresh wooden beams erected as temporary supports. A hush lingered as Master Zhang unrolled the scroll one final time.

He read the prophecy's lines once more, letting each syllable echo. "'Its light shall bring balance to the world, but only in the hands of those chosen to protect it.'"

Then Master Zhang set the scroll aside, turning to Jeremy, Lucas, and Sophia. "This temple recognizes you as the diamond's rightful guardians. Will you honor that duty—protecting it from greed, using it for the world's well-being?"

Mr. Zhang stood slightly behind his elder brother, arms folded, proud but calm. "You have shown bravery, but it must continue. The world beyond these mountains remains in chaos."

Jeremy exchanged glances with Lucas and Sophia. He swallowed, heart pounding from the weight of the vow. "We accept. We'll protect the diamond and do our best to restore balance, however we can."

Sophia and Lucas nodded in unison, each placing a hand lightly on the diamond's silk-wrapped form. The gem glimmered, a soft wave of luminescence rolling over its surface. A hush fell, as though the temple and the mountain itself acknowledged their oath.

When the vow was spoken, a sense of quiet resolution settled in their hearts. No fanfare or cosmic sign signaled the prophecy's fulfillment, just the measured faith in each other and in the diamond's mysterious power. They parted ways to continue the day's tasks, but a new unity bound them—the chosen protectors.

Late that evening, after hours of labor, they reconvened near a rebuilt section of the courtyard. Lanterns hung from makeshift poles, illuminating weary monks finishing their chores. Jeremy, Lucas, Sophia, and both Zhang brothers sank onto improvised seats, sore muscles craving rest.

"We've started," Lucas said, voice tinged with cautious optimism. "Who knows how many more threats are out there—but at least we have a direction."

Sophia closed her eyes for a moment, exhaustion visible on her features. "I'm just relieved we're not alone. This place, these monks ... I feel like we're part of something bigger than ourselves now."

Jeremy exhaled slowly, gaze lingering on the diamond, which lay nearby on a folded mat. A faint pulse of color rippled across its surface. "We are. And it's not just about big battles, is it? It's about everyday acts that bring balance. Whether it's saving a village from lava or saving a temple from bullets."

Mr. Zhang offered a small but genuine smile, leaning back against a repaired column. "Exactly. The prophecy demands not just warriors, but stewards of compassion."

Master Zhang, arms resting on his knees, studied the star-flecked sky overhead. "Tonight, we rest. Tomorrow, we continue rebuilding. Beyond that, the diamond's path remains uncertain. But you will walk it willingly."

Jeremy nodded, placing a hand near the gem's shimmering surface without quite touching it. "We'll see it through, no matter what."

Chapter 15

The sun dipped low over the temple's ancient walls, bathing the half-reconstructed structure in an otherworldly glow. Warm gold rays slanted across the courtyard, illuminating piles of stone and timber that villagers and monks alike had gathered. Over the past days, they had worked tirelessly, determined to restore what Sergei's assault had nearly destroyed. Hammers clanged against chisels, voices rose in spirited collaboration, and despite the lingering scars— shattered pillars, scorched rooftops—hope pulsed through the temple like a newly invigorated heartbeat.

Near the central courtyard, Jeremy carefully tightened the straps of his backpack. Inside it lay the diamond, its soft glow muted under layers of cloth. Even concealed, he could feel its gentle hum, reminding him of the power it held—and the responsibility it entailed. He inhaled the mountain air, still tinged with the faint aroma of burnt incense, and exhaled a mixture of relief and sadness. *We're really leaving*, he thought.

A few steps away, Lucas sat in his wheelchair, hands resting on the emperor's sword balanced across his lap. The blade's jade-encrusted hilt glistened in the late-afternoon light. His expression flickered between awe and the weight of duty. Ever since he had summoned the Chinese dragon to defend the temple, the sword had bonded with him in an inexplicable yet undeniable way.

Master Zhang approached, his crimson and gold robes stirring in the breeze, the faint lines of exhaustion on his face betraying the grueling days of post-battle work. He stopped beside Lucas, placing a hand on the younger man's shoulder. "The sword belongs with you now," he said, voice low but resonant. "You will need the strength it offers to maintain the balance we spoke of."

Lucas managed a small grin. "So, no dragon included in this package? Just a fancy sword?"

A soft laugh rumbled in Master Zhang's chest. "The dragon is bound to the sword's magic. If ever the world shakes again, and you prove worthy, its spirit will heed your call. Until then, keep your intentions pure and your heart humble."

Lucas nodded, his teasing smile tempered by seriousness. "Right. Guess I'd better stay on its good side."

Master Zhang walked over to his brother, who stood on the temple steps a short distance away. They embraced—a private moment between siblings who had endured both war and reconciliation. Master Zhang's posture was both proud and reluctant, as if torn between relief at their success and worry about the trials ahead.

"Are you certain you should leave so soon?" Master Zhang asked, his voice tinged with concern. "These young ones have only just stepped onto this path. The diamond's power draws chaos like moths to a flame, as we've seen."

Mr. Zhang offered a gentle, reassuring smile. "They're ready, brother. More than you think. And I'll be alongside them."

Master Zhang's gaze wandered to the monks and villagers hauling stone blocks along a makeshift ramp. "Work here is vital. The spirit of the temple must endure for future generations. Our fallen monks' sacrifices can't be forgotten."

His brother nodded. "What you rebuild stands as a testament for centuries, a place of healing for those yet to be born. People will remember this place not for the destruction, but for the resilience and harmony it embodies."

Master Zhang allowed himself a thin, proud smile. "You always had a knack for seeing the larger picture, even when you tried to outrun it by cooking noodles in America."

A wry chuckle escaped Mr. Zhang's lips. "I wanted to be a simple chef. Funny how destiny had other plans."

Master Zhang's expression grew somber. "You have shaped Jeremy's will and skill. He may become the greatest warrior of our time if he keeps his heart centered. But be warned: the diamond's full potential isn't yet revealed. Sergei was only a minor ripple. Larger storms await."

Mr. Zhang gripped his brother's arm in a brief, firm gesture of respect. "Then we'll face those storms. One day, one choice at a time."

Meanwhile, Jeremy and Lucas hovered near the temple's edge, where the mountains dropped off into a panorama of rolling clouds and winding trails. Sophia, quiet but ever present, stood with them, her calm gaze reflecting the orange glow of the sinking sun.

"Are you ready to go back home?" Jeremy asked, glancing at Lucas.

Lucas let out a soft chuckle, eyes flicking to the sword. "I never thought standing up to bullies in Crescent Bay would lead to all this," he said, gesturing at the remnants of ancient walls, the scaffolding, and the sword resting on his lap. "A lonely, disabled kid becomes … what, the emperor's sword-bearer?"

Jeremy shrugged, returning a grin. "Has a ring to it. 'Lucas Chu, Sword Keeper Extraordinaire.' Right up there with 'Jeremy Carter, Surfer Ninja.'"

A gentle snort escaped Lucas. "Don't forget I owe it all to you. You were the first who believed I had more in me than people saw. Now I've summoned a mythical dragon. No big deal."

Jeremy gave him a friendly nudge. "Sure you want to remind yourself of that? The next time you try it, who knows how big it'll get."

Sophia folded her arms, smiling at their banter. "You two are hopeless. Good thing I'm around to keep you grounded."

A thoughtful pause followed, the sun dipping another notch behind the peaks. Jeremy's expression shifted from playful to earnest. "This path is bigger than any of us imagined. I wanted just to ride waves and be a pro surfer. Now I'm … something else."

Sophia laid a hand on his shoulder. "You're still you. None of us asked for this, but we can't deny what we've accomplished."

Lucas added quietly, "And we're a weirdly effective team, for sure."

Jeremy let out a breath, turning to admire the last sliver of sunlight. "So, let's see it through, yeah?"

Sophia nodded; Lucas, too. A sense of camaraderie warmed the moment, forging the next step of their collective journey.

***

When the sun finally vanished beyond the ridges, they began their departure. The battered temple courtyard shimmered under torchlight, monks bowing in silent farewell. Some villagers, still carrying beams and masonry, paused to wave timidly. Master Zhang and Mr. Zhang stood near the main gate, each clasping an arm in a final, solemn goodbye.

Mr. Zhang stepped aside to join Jeremy, Lucas, and Sophia. With a final glance at the temple—its half-rebuilt arches and scaffolding silhouetted against the twilight—he led them down the ancient stone path. The flicker of torches receded behind them as they wound their way down the mountain track, hearts full of gratitude and resolve.

They traveled by cart through the winding foothills, then boarded a modest bus to the nearest city. From there, the group took a high-speed train, the bullet-nosed locomotive slicing through valleys and farmland at dizzying speeds. During that ride, they all dozed intermittently, the hum of tracks lulling them into a sense of uneasy rest. Jeremy kept the diamond stowed, Lucas kept the emperor's sword sheathed in a discreet traveling case, and Sophia eyed the passing countryside, pondering what new trials awaited them.

Eventually, they caught a flight back to Crescent Bay. The tension in the plane was palpable, each of them flipping through thoughts of the prophecy, the diamond's precarious power, and how to guard it in the modern world.

The plane touched down at Crescent Bay's modest airport. As they stepped onto the tarmac, salt-tinged air greeted them like an old friend. The bustling city lights twinkled in the distance; the surf pounded somewhere out of sight. Despite their new purpose, a familiarity in the coastal wind welcomed them home.

They rented a van for the short drive through the city's patchwork of highways. Buildings soared in neon gleams, while the ocean horizon glistened under a half-moon. Jeremy felt an odd pang of nostalgia, recalling simpler times at the beach, free from cosmic responsibilities. Yet the diamond's comforting warmth in his bag reminded him that such normalcy was gone, or at least deeply altered.

Lucas stared out the van's window, gazing at Crescent Bay's skyline. "Feels weird, being back, huh? Like we left a different life behind."

Sophia nodded in the front seat. "And we come back changed people."

Mr. Zhang, driving with calm concentration, simply said, "That's the nature of journeys with the Tao. You return, yet everything is different. Including yourself."

Jeremy exchanged a small smile with Lucas. Their eyes flicked to the precious cargo each carried: the diamond and the emperor's sword, cornerstones of a grand destiny none of them had asked for.

Night had fully descended by the time they reached the lab—the place where so much had started for Lucas and Jeremy. The building looked mostly unchanged from the outside: a nondescript structure near a quiet side street. Illuminated by a single fluorescent sign, it seemed deserted at this hour.

Jeremy hopped out of the van, backpack slung over one shoulder. He guided Lucas's wheelchair up the short ramp, Sophia close behind. Mr. Zhang followed, scanning the surroundings with that martial awareness he never lost. The door lock beeped as Lucas keyed in a code, letting them inside.

They entered an open expanse of half-finished projects and battered equipment. Shelves sagged under old prototypes and circuit boards, while the distinctive tang of soldered metal clung to the stale air. Flicking on the overhead fluorescents, they discovered the lab … mostly as they'd left it. Except for one unsettling detail.

A tall figure in a perfectly tailored black suit stood in the middle of the room, back turned. Shadows played across his shoulders, and he held a sleek phone in one hand.

Jeremy froze, adrenaline spiking. "Who—?"

The stranger pivoted languidly, blond hair styled immaculately, dark sunglasses reflecting the glaring overhead lights. He wore an expression that hovered between confident and condescending.

"Jeremy Carter. Lucas Chu. Miss Sokolova, Mr. Zhang," the man greeted them, voice smooth as polished stone. "I've been waiting for you."

Jeremy Carter: The Swell of Hope and Fury

Jeremy's muscles tensed, the weight of the diamond in his bag suddenly more acute. "Who the hell are you?"

A faint, knowing smile curled the man's lips. "You can call me Mr. Grey. I represent … certain interests that have been watching your escapades."

Lucas's brow furrowed. "Watching us? For how long?"

Mr. Grey adjusted his tie, stepping away from a table cluttered with electronics. "Let's say we became intrigued after certain events surfaced on camera. A dragon in China, for instance. Very impressive—and very troubling, from a certain perspective."

Sophia's arms crossed protectively. "You broke into our lab?"

Mr. Grey shrugged, unperturbed. "I found the door unlocked. Perhaps you were in a hurry when you left. My presence here is a courtesy, I assure you."

A quiet beat settled. Jeremy felt Mr. Zhang shift behind him, the older man clearly ready for confrontation if needed. But Mr. Grey didn't advance. He merely watched them with an unsettling calm.

"Footage? Of the temple fight?" Sophia asked, her voice edgy. "Who else knows?"

Grey pressed his lips together in a ghost of a smile. "The short answer: many. But let's not get ahead of ourselves. I'm here to make an offer."

An uneasy energy sparked in the air. Jeremy's mind raced, imagining all the worst-case scenarios: more clandestine agents, more attempts to harness the diamond or the sword. "What kind of offer?" he demanded.

Mr. Grey's smile widened, revealing pristine teeth. "Let's talk," he said simply.

Author Profile

Lior Zelering is a versatile figure, excelling as an author, designer, product manager and digital media expert. He founded Masters Design Lab and has taught at various design institutions. With a diverse portfolio, Lior has written and edited books on design software, intellectual property protection, surfing, and more. He's also contributed to magazines and online publications covering design, multimedia, and skateboarding.

***

What Did You Think of *Jeremy Carter: The Swell of Hope and Fury?*

A big thank you for purchasing this book. It means a lot that you chose this book specifically from such a wide range on offer. I do hope you enjoyed it.

Book reviews are incredibly important for an author. All feedback helps them improve their writing for future projects and for developing this edition. If you are able to spare a few minutes to post a review on Amazon, that would be much appreciated.

Publisher Information

Rowanvale Books provides publishing services to independent authors, writers and poets all over the globe. We deliver a personal, honest and efficient service that allows authors to see their work published, while remaining in control of the process and retaining their creativity. By making publishing services available to authors in a cost-effective and ethical way, we at Rowanvale Books hope to ensure that the local, national and international community benefits from a steady stream of good quality literature.

For more information about us, our authors or our publications, please get in touch.

www.rowanvalebooks.com
info@rowanvalebooks.com